a Story of Love

Secret of What Matters Most

Marsha Sabin Pester

Cover & interior design by Typewriter Creative Co.
Cover images by preto_perola, LiliGraphie, and fruitcocktail via Adobe Stock.
Interior graphics by Freepik.com.

ISBN 979-8-9871053-4-4 (Paperback)
ISBN 979-8-9871053-5-1 (eBook)

Dedication

To John, my best friend.

 **Chapter 1**

"Mother, please, stop crying. Your eyes are going to be all red and puffy."

"June, I just can't help it. You don't know that man Frank, all that well and you're moving miles away. The way times are, who knows when or how often we'll be able to see each other."

June sighed and smiled at her mother. It was June's wedding day, June 18, 1938. Three days before, June had turned twenty-four. Her mother, Della Witherspoon, had named her daughter for the month of her birth. June used to joke with her mother, she was fortunate, she hadn't been born in a month like February or October. Her mother couldn't see the humor in it.

The words of her mother reverberated in June's mind. If she were honest, she really did not know a lot about her fiancé, Frank Grimes. She knew he was a widower and a traveling salesman for the R&R Brothers Grocery Supply Company. He had lived all his life in Fairview, a town about 150 miles from Ravensburg, where June had grown up.

Frank had told her a little about his family. His father, Art Grimes, was also an employee at R&R and very well liked. Frank said he knew he had been hired only because of the trust the owners had in his dad. He worked hard at his job to prove he deserved the same trust.

Two weeks ago, Art had been injured while

working in the packing department. An unbalanced stack of boxes containing canned goods had toppled on him. He suffered a collapsed lung and several broken ribs. He was still recovering from those injuries and, as yet, had not returned to work. For this reason, Frank's family would not be coming to the wedding.

Frank's route normally took him to Ravensburg a couple of times a month. He and June had met three years ago in Crosby's Friendly Foods Grocery Store, down the street from the Witherspoon home. Frank had been trying to convince Mr. Crosby who was standing behind the cash register, to order a new kind of liquid dish soap. Liquid soap had just come onto the market. Most housewives shaved thin slivers off a large bar of soap or used laundry detergent to wash dishes.

June had stood off to one side enjoying the banter between the two men. The owner finally acquiesced and ordered a half case.

Frank had noticed June watching him as he was writing up the order. She was a looker! He figured June to be in her early twenties, not real slim but not heavy either. Like the story of "Goldilocks and the Three Bears", she was 'just right'. She had a pleasing oval face with high cheek bones, and full lips. Her hair was done in the latest shoulder-length pageboy style, popularized by Greta Garbo. The freckles across her nose, along with a becoming tan, made him think she must enjoy being outdoors. He was not sure of the color of her eyes until the cloud obscuring the sun moved on. Bright light emanated through the front window revealing to him her kind blue eyes behind wire-rimmed glasses. A bit of cheek rouge and lipstick was her only make-up.

Her dress of blue and white seersucker was all business but fit her very well. He wondered if she was a secretary.

June was sizing up Frank at the same time he was assessing her. He looked to be in his late twenties or early thirties. Wondering if he was married, she glanced at his left hand. She did not see a ring on his finger, but a lot of men did not wear wedding bands. Handsome with wavy light brown hair, combed straight back, he was about as tall as her oldest brother, Carl, five feet eight or nine inches. He was a little on the heavy side. Doubtless, he did not get enough exercise driving from town to town all the time and daily eating in restaurants.

June looked out of the front window at Frank's car. Everyone in town knew this car. It was a 1934, V-8 Ford, Deluxe. It was the same model Bonnie and Clyde had been in when they were shot and killed in May of that same year. Frank's car was dark blue. June thought, "How I would love to have a ride in that car!"

"Do you like my car?" At first June did not realize Frank was talking to her. "I said, do you like my car? Would you like a ride?"

June turned to look at Frank, "Excuse me. Are you talking to me?"

"Well, I don't see anyone else around. My name's Frank Grimes and that's my car. Want to go for a spin around town?"

June stood mesmerized looking into Frank's deep set, soft brown eyes. He had a long slender nose and a very prominent jaw line. Not sure how to respond, June stood looking at Frank. Really wanting a ride, and wanting to get better acquainted with this man, June, however, knew it might be considered improper. She had just been hired to start her first year of teaching in September, at a one-room school about eight miles out of town. What would a member of the school board say if he saw them riding around?

Finally, she found her tongue. To her astonishment she replied, "Yes, I would."

"Well, come on then. My friends call me Frank. By-the-way, what's your name?"

So began the three-year courtship of June and Frank. June's parents did not like Frank, mainly because he was a traveling salesman. This meant he only came to town occasionally. And for all anyone knew; Frank could have a girlfriend in every other town. June said that was ridiculous. As their love blossomed, he began to visit more frequently, arriving in the evenings after finishing his business in one of the nearby towns.

Frank was thirty-one and a widower. He didn't talk much about this first marriage and June did not press him about it. All he said was that they had both been young. She was just a teen-ager and Frank was twenty. He had started working as a salesman shortly before their wedding. This necessitated his traveling from Monday morning to Friday afternoon of each week.

During the ensuing three years of June and Frank's courtship, he volunteered more information about his first wife. Millicent had died of a ruptured appendix, alone in their house, unable to summon help. Frank told June he felt responsible for her death because she had asked him to have a telephone installed. She was afraid of living in the house by herself. He insisted they could not afford one.

At that time, the country was in the grip of a great depression. It was being strangled. The downturn in the economy had started in 1929. It was the harshest financial collapse in modern history. Hundreds of banks failed, causing investors as well as savers to lose all their assets. Factories closed and millions of people were laid-off. Those fortunate enough to retain their jobs saw their income shrink by a third. This had included Frank.

He told Millicent he was barely making enough to pay what bills they already had. And besides, Millicent was only a short distance from their nearest neighbor. They also had a watch dog to protect her. He had never imagined such a tragedy, as a ruptured appendix, would happen to his teen-aged wife.

Chapter 2

June 18, 1938, turned out to be a perfect day for a wedding. The temperature was in the low 80s with a slight breeze. The ceremony was held outdoors and had been lovely. Mrs. Witherspoon cried throughout the entire service.

June wore her paternal grandmother's wedding gown. It had been altered to fit her. Made of off-white satin with long sleeves and a high neck line, it was very warm. June was wearing a commercial antiperspirant for the first time. She was glad her mother had given it to her and insisted she wear it.

The roses she carried were from her maternal grandmother's garden. Two days before the wedding the roses were barely more than buds. Grandmother assured the florist who was to arrange the bridal bouquet, the roses would be blooming perfectly for the wedding. They were.

June came down the aisle. The first thing she saw was Frank's wide smile. He looked so handsome in his new black pin-striped suit. It was doubled-breasted with wide lapels. The trousers were pleated with wide cuffs. His hair was slicked back. She thought he was the finest-looking man she had ever seen.

Observing June walking with her father, Frank's heart swelled. He couldn't believe, he was really marrying this lovely woman. Her face was shrouded by the white veil but he knew behind it was a special person.

The Witherspoon home was large with extended gardens and lawn. The wedding ceremony was performed in a wisteria covered garden area. After the nuptials, a reception luncheon was served on a terraced veranda which led down to a tree shaded park like area. Frank was polite and congenial to the guests. But he really was anxious to get out of his very hot suit and leave for the honeymoon.

The couple drove for almost three hours, glad at last to be alone. Frank hadn't told June where they were going. He wanted to surprise her. Surprise was hardly the word. Just after five o'clock, they stopped at Tom and Jane's Auto Court. June saw six or eight white cabins in a line beside a large white house. Frank stopped the car on the gravel driveway, "This is one of the places I stay at when I'm in this area. The owners are real nice. Come on, I'll introduce you to them."

Frank reached over and opened the door on June's side then got out on the driver's side of the car. Tom and Jane were walking up to the car as the newlyweds exited. They were of middle age with graying hair. Tom was short and round. He had a huge smile below a tiny pencil thin mustache. He was missing a front tooth. His eyes sparkled with mischief. Tom shook Frank's hand, "Well, good afternoon to the happy couple! Frank, you sure got yourself a pretty bride. Ain't she lovely Jane?"

"Why she's even prettier than you described to us. I fixed up number six, like you asked. It's all ready for you." Jane was grinning from ear to ear. Her complexion was smooth and pink. Unlike her husband, she was tall and fragile looking.

"Thanks Jane. Honey, this is Jane and Tom House. This is my bride, June. Let's walk to the cottage. I'll bring the car down later."

June had never stayed in an auto court. She did not know what to expect. Frank opened the door for her. She walked a couple of steps into the room and stopped. She saw a bed covered with a blue and yellow chenille spread. A small night stand stood next to one side. It held a small lamp and a radio. In the middle of the room was a very small table with two chairs. A small chest of drawers was on the opposite wall to the bed. Over it was a very small mirror.

"I hope this is okay. I thought you might like to stay in one of the places I stay when I'm traveling. Each Monday before I leave, I plan to give you a list of what towns I'll be traveling to and where I'm staying. That way you can get in touch with me if necessary."

"Yes, that would be good. Where is the bathroom?

"Come outside, I'll show you." June followed Frank out to the small porch. "See the big house? That's were Tom and Jane live. See the long building just behind it? On one side is the ladies' showers and facilities. The other side is the men's. It's a bit of a walk. But you'll only need to go there a couple of times a day. So, it won't be too bad." They returned to the cabin.

"Are we planning to eat all our meals out?"

"Just lunch and supper. For an extra quarter each, Jane will bring our breakfast to us. We just need to let her know what time."

The breakfast, Sunday morning, consisted of cold, hard cooked eggs, unbuttered toast, and coffee. June ate one egg and one slice of toast. Frank asked if that was all she was having. She told him it was. He finished his two eggs and toast then ate her second egg and toast.

Neither Jane nor Frank mentioned going to church. Regular church attendance was not their habit. They spent the pleasant day driving to three different towns. Frank introduced June to several people in each town. He talked a lot about his job. They ate lunch in a diner at the edge of one of the towns. It was not the kind of honeymoon June had envisioned. Frank did take June to an elegant restaurant at the edge of a charming lake.

June felt underdressed and grubby after spending all day driving around. Most of the other ladies were in evening clothes and the male patrons were in suits. Frank did not seem to notice.

Monday morning after a breakfast of barely warm pancakes, one sausage link each and coffee, Frank told June to put on her swim suit under her clothes. June had bought a new suit for the honeymoon. The green paisley swimsuit was two-pieced, consisting of a To…halter top tied around the neck and back. When Mrs. Witherspoon had seen the suit she said, "It looks like you have on a bra and underpants. Well, at least your navel is covered." Frank said he really liked it. Over the suit, June decided to wear shorts and a sheer blouse. This also met with her husband's approval.

Frank had arranged with Mrs. House to pack a picnic lunch. They drove to the opposite side of the lake where they had dined the day before. The day was spent swimming, walking around in the woods, and resting on a blanket while enjoying each other's company. June read Frank from her favorite poetry book. He fell asleep.

Chapter 3

The newlyweds arrived at his house Tuesday afternoon. He had not told June much about his house or the town of Fairview. June's heart sank as they pulled into the driveway. The front door of the house was literally steps from the dirt road and across from the railroad tracks. Before the car had stopped a passenger train came roaring by, going south. This train had scarcely passed when a freight train thundered through on a north bound track. June sat in the passenger's seat staring out the windshield, dumbfounded.

Frank looked at a worried June, "Don't even

think about the trains. You'll get used to them. In time you'll hardly notice." June doubted that. "Look, there's my mom and dad and my sister and her husband."

Emerging from the front door were a group of smiling people. The woman who June figured was Frank's sister, was holding a baby. Another child peeked bashfully around from behind her skirt. Frank did not wait for June to get out of the car nor did he come around to her side to help her out. He jumped out and started for the porch. Before he had taken four steps a huge long-haired black dog of unknown heritage came bounding down the steps. It jumped on Frank putting its massive paws on Frank's shoulders licking his face and almost knocking him over. June knew the dog was named Baxter and had been Frank's for several years.

"Okay Bax, okay! Get down. I'm glad to see you too." Frank pushed Baxter away from him, giving the dog hugs and pats as Baxter remained standing close to his master.

June just sat in the car. Then she noticed the older woman smiling at her and starting to walk towards the car. June jumped out of the passenger's side and walked briskly up to the house.

"Hello June. I'm Hilda Grimes, Frank's mother." Hilda was slender with short permed gray hair. Smiling at June she continued, "Baxter is sure happy to have Frank home."

"Oh, I'm sorry." Frank took June by the hand, "Folks, this is my new bride, June. June, this is my dad, Art, my mom, Hilda, my sister Ruth and her husband Duke Pember. The baby is Milo and that youngster hiding behind his mom is Everett." The dog growled at June. "Easy Bax. This is your new mistress. Don't be afraid June. He'll get used to you. He's your protector." June wondered if she would get used to Baxter.

The others had come off the porch and were standing around. June glanced at Frank's father, Art. Frank was a younger version of his father, except Frank still had hair. June wondered if at his father's age would Frank still have his hair.

Ruth had the harried look of a weary young mother. Her hair was covered with a man's red bandana. It was folded into a triangle and tied at the back of her neck, under her hair. The dress she wore was tight and gapped at the buttons over her breasts. Another train roared by.

Ruth's husband, Duke, grabbed Frank's

hand and was giving him a hearty handshake. June noticed his huge hands. They appeared to know physical labor. A heavy five o'clock shadow was in evidence on his rather handsome face.

Hilda took June's hand, "Let's go inside so we can hear each other talk." The entourage, including Baxter, moved into the front room of the house.

Neither Frank, nor anyone else, said anything about carrying June across the threshold. She was glad because she would have been embarrassed.

June was aghast as she surveyed the living room, which was wallpapered with large red roses. If she had thought the honeymoon cabin was primitive, this appeared to be much worse.

It was very crowded with all the people

in it. An empty wood-burning stove took up a large part of the area. A very worn linoleum rug covered most of the floor. June guessed the rug was about nine feet by twelve feet. Subflooring could be seen around the edges of the room. The subflooring showed evidence of once having been painted white. Ruth and her children sat down on a tattered green sofa. Her husband grabbed the only other piece of furniture, a dark brown, run-down, over-stuffed chair. Across from these two pieces of furniture was a large chest commonly referred to as a hope chest. On top of it sat a radio, a telephone and an 8x10 picture of an extremely beautiful young woman. June knew immediately, it was Millicent, Frank's first wife.

Ruth pulled Everett off the couch saying, "Son, get up. Let your grandpa sit down. You know he isn't well." Art took the offered seat and motioned for Everett to come sit on his lap. June stood just inside the door unnerved by the nearness of the train tracks, the new relatives, and the gaudy decor. She loved Frank with all her heart. But all this at once was difficult to grasp.

"Honey, did you hear what Mom said?"

"What? I'm sorry."

Hilda spoke again, "All of this must be overwhelming to you. I made supper for you." Smiling warmly, she continued, "I hope chicken and dumplings are satisfactory. It's keeping warm in the oven."

June turned to her mother-in-law, "That sounds lovely. Thank you."

"I've also put some items in the cupboard that I thought you might need tonight. I'm sure you'll need to go to the store. If you want, I can come by tomorrow about nine to take you."

"Yes, that would be very kind of you. Thank you."

"Well, folks, let's get going. These newlyweds probably want to be alone." Art had spoken for the first time.

With hugs and kisses, everyone left. Hilda promised to come by about nine the next morning. June and Frank were left standing in the front room staring at each other.

"I hope you're not too disappointed. I know the house isn't much. Millicent and I had made big plans on how to improve the place. Then she died and I just sort 'a gave up. But, now you're here, we can fix up the place. After supper I'll show you the paper Millicent wrote. It lists what she thought should be done. First, let me show you the rest of the house."

Directly off the front room was the only bedroom. The couple walked into it and stopped. Facing them was a single bed. "Those jerks! I ordered a new bedroom set for you. The Duly's Furniture people promised to have it here by this morning. I'll give'm a call."

Frank returned to the living room to use the telephone. After Millicent's death, he had one installed. June could hear him talking as she looked around the bedroom. This room was also wallpapered, only in large yellow roses. There was no closet. On either side of the front window were pegs. Hanging on the pegs on one side were a couple of pieces of men's clothing. The pegs on the other side were empty. Against the back wall was a small chest of drawers. The floor was covered with another worn linoleum rug. This one had been haphazardly cut smaller to fit the room.

Coming back into the bedroom, Frank told June, "Mr. Duly said he'll be here within the hour with the furniture. When Millicent died, I gave our bedroom set to Ruth and Duke. They had just gotten married and needed a bed. I couldn't bring myself to sleep in that bed anymore.

"I hope you'll like the new set. It's golden oak. Millicent saw it in the store window, and at once, she wanted us to buy it. I told her I would, after things got a little better financially for us. Come on, I'll show you the kitchen." June followed behind Frank wondering, "What next?"

The kitchen was the largest room in the house taking up the entire south side of the building. The floor was painted subflooring. Under a south window was a dry sink. Next to it was a short-handled cistern pump. In the middle of the room stood a large oak table, covered with a worn, red, and yellow flowered oil cloth.

As wedding gifts, the couple had received six sets of table linens. Two of the table cloths were hand crocheted. One set of linens was from Ireland and included twelve dinner napkins. June sadly looked around and decided, she would not be giving any dinner parties in this house. The table linens along with silver candle sticks could remain packed.

June felt heat radiating from a black wood-burning cookstove. On the opposite wall from the stove was a Hoosier cupboard. June had a childhood friend whose mother had a Hoosier cupboard in her kitchen.

This cupboard appeared to have seen better days. It was a dirty white color with a small work surface and bins for storing kitchen equipment. It also had several racks for holding spices. June only saw two spices, salt and pepper. She knew the upper doors on either side opened and had bins for storing flour and sugar. Sitting at the back of the cupboard was a glass jar holding coffee.

So, this was the whole house. June, all at once realized there was no running water or indoor plumbing in the house. How could she ever live in such a place?

June had grown up in relative luxury. Her childhood home was a large brick six-bedroom house with three bathrooms. Two maids and a cook were employed full-time. June had done very little cooking or house work. Her father had a valet that doubled as the butler. A gardener was employed part-time.

"Where do we take a bath? How do the clothes get washed?"

"Honey, like I said, it's not much. Let's eat supper and afterwards I'll show you the plans Millicent made."

"How do I go to the bathroom?"

"It's outside."

"OUTSIDE?"

Frank pointed to a small building in the backyard. "It's called an outhouse. Haven't you ever used one when you were camping or on a picnic?"

"I've never been camping except for the couple of days on our honeymoon. My family only went on picnics at my grandparents' or uncles' homes. We were always close enough to their homes to use the facilities inside."

"What about at your school? Wasn't it only one room?"

"The school had been built to be used as a community gathering place. People used it for meetings, wedding receptions, dances and other events. There were two bathrooms, one for boys and the other for girls. There was also a small kitchenette. I could have lived there if I had wanted to."

"Oh, ah, there's one more thing. Don't drink any water from the indoor pump. It's rain water off the roof." Frank walked to the back door and pointed to a pump in the middle of the backyard. "That pump there is a deep-water pump." He then walked to the dry sink and picked up a large metal container. "You'll need to fill this from the outside pump to use for drinking and cooking.

"Don't worry you'll get used to everything, eventually. Millicent did." June doubted she would get used to living here, nor did she want to. Just then another train roared by. "Look, Mom made a cherry pie. She knows it's my favorite. She taught Millicent how to make pies. I know she'll be glad to teach you too. Let's eat." June had lost her appetite.

At 8:00 p.m. Duly's Furniture delivery truck backed into the driveway. Charles Duly was the third owner of the business. His grandfather had started out as an undertaker and casket maker. He made furniture when business was slow. His son, Charles Junior came into the business encouraging his father to discontinue undertaking and concentrate on furniture.

By the time Charles Senior retired, Charles the third was working for the company. They were no longer making any furniture only selling quality brand pieces.

The Duly company was able to weather the depression better than other establishments. It was an old company and the family owned their building. The sale of new furniture had been low during the worst of the time; but was beginning to pick up.

Charles Duly the third, delivered the set himself, apologizing for being so late. Frank helped Mr. Duly carry the furniture in. June had to admit the bedroom set was lovely. There was a double bed, mattress, and bed springs, a large chest of drawers and a beautiful vanity including a large round mirror with a covered stool. After the new set had been arranged, there was scarcely any room left in the bedroom to walk.

Mr. Duly gave the newlyweds a wedding present as he was leaving, a set of bed linens. They smiled and thanked him.
He did not know the back seat and trunk of their car was filled with wedding and shower presents. Included in the gifts were five sets of bed linens.

Chapter 4

June didn't get much sleep that night. Train after train went by. It was bad enough that they made so much noise and everything in the house shook. How could Frank ever have bought such an awful house! Worse yet, was his continued reference to Millicent. June wondered, "What was she to do?" She really did love Frank. Aside from what he expected her to live in, there was a dark unseen shadow between them. That shadow was Millicent.

She finally dozed off just as the night cartwheeled into dawn, only to be once more awakened. This time it was Baxter's barking. The barking was coming from the backyard. Slowly she got up and trudged to the kitchen. Oh! She was going to have to go outside to that wretched, smelly building. Another train rumbled by. She didn't think this one was ever going to get past. It got slower and slower, finally the caboose stopped just beyond the house.

She knew it was going to be a hot June day. The kitchen was already insufferable. The cookstove was blazing away.

Out in the yard Baxter continued to bark. She saw a young man running across the yard with Baxter close behind. Frank came up to the porch from the outhouse. "And stay out of here! Don't ever come in this yard again or my dog will have you for breakfast!" Having said that he let Baxter into the house and followed him in.

"What was that all about?"

"It was one of the bums from the train. It's not unusual for one or two to stop by daily, asking for something to eat. Baxter usually scares them off before they get to the house."

"Everyday?"

"Yeah, you don't have to worry. Like I said, Baxter takes care of them. If any do make it to the house, make sure you never, ever hand out any food. No matter how sincere they are or what kind of a sob-story they tell you, don't give them anything. If you do, the house will be marked and there'll be men begging at the door constantly."

"Who looked after the house and dog all week when you weren't here?"

Frank bent over and gave his wife a kiss. "My brother-in-law, Duke, goes right by here on his way to work. He has been stopping by in the morning to feed Baxter and made sure he has water. On his way home he stops again to pick up the mail and check on Baxter. I pay him a couple of bucks a week for doing it. I guess he won't have to do that anymore, now that you're here.

"I made some coffee. I had a slice of Mom's pie for breakfast. I'm not sure what else there is. Do you want a slice?"

"No, coffee is enough for now. I have to go outside first. Do you think the man is gone?"

"Probably. I'll send Baxter out with you. He'll look after you."

June looked at Baxter who stared back. She thought he looked like he would rather eat her for breakfast than protect her. As she walked to the outhouse, June thought,

"This place isn't even as modern as the honeymoon cabin. At least there, at the end of the walk, were real showers and toilets. Not a board with a hole."

When June returned, a cup of black coffee sat on the table. She could hear Frank in the bedroom. June washed her hands at the dry sink which held a pan of water. She picked up the coffee and went outdoors. She hated this place. No wonder Frank had been reluctant to tell her about it. And if she heard the name of his first wife mentioned once more, she thought she would scream. She wondered when Frank made love to her, who was he thinking about.

Before Frank left for work, he carried the boxes containing their wedding gifts into the house. They were scattered in all three rooms. Frank put the last box down and looked around. "Ya know, it might be a good idea for you to go through these boxes. We probably don't need all this stuff right now. I'm sure my folks would let us store some of the boxes in their basement." June agreed.

Frank would be gone three days, until Friday afternoon. June began taking items out of the boxes and finding places to put them which was difficult. Her parents had given her a set of China dishes, crystal stemware and silverware. She didn't unpack them. She thought there was no use. Then she remembered, her mother-in-law would soon be by to take her to the store.

June went into the bedroom and took out a dress from her suitcase. It was too wrinkled to wear. Searching for several minutes she finally found her iron. There was no ironing board so she put a towel on the table. This worked out well as the only electrical outlet was hanging down from the ceiling in the middle of the table. It was next to the light that was also hanging above the table. She stood in her slip and underclothes ironing the dress. Baxter raised his head. He had been dozing on the back porch. Then he began to bark. June dashed to the bedroom and put on her dress.

Baxter was now barking loudly. "It's okay boy. I'm not going to hurt you. Is your mistress around?" June returned to the kitchen and saw a shabby bent-over man standing at the foot of the porch steps. He was trying to pet Baxter, who was now growling. June glanced at the hook and eye lock on the screen door. It was not latched. The coffee pot still sat on the hot stove. She picked up the pot to use as a weapon, if necessary, then walked casually to the door and quickly slipped the hook through the eye.

"What do you want? You'd better leave before my dog bites you."

"Now, ma'am, I ain't gonna hurt you. I saw your husband leave". He said this with a smirk. "I just want a bite to eat. Surely you can spare a few crumbs for a poor hungry man." The hobo started up the steps as Baxter snarled.

"Get him, Baxter!" Hearing June's command, Baxter sprang at the bum. The man turned and ran with Baxter at his heels. June thought, "For an old man he sure can run fast. Probably he's not as old as he appears. Just road weary! What would he have done if he had gotten into the house?" June was sure she knew the answer.

She carried a chair from the kitchen to the front porch. With cars going by, she felt safe from being bothered by tramps. The radio announcer had said the temperature at 8:30 was 88°.

Hilda arrived just after nine o'clock. Her mother-in-law, wearing a white and yellow gingham dress, looked cool and comfortable. "Today is going to be a scorcher. I was wondering if you would like to drive around town before we shop? It will help you get to know the town better."

"Oh, yes. I really would appreciate that."

"Also, do you have any dirty clothes? It will be very difficult to wash them here. You're welcome to bring them to my house each week. I normally wash on Mondays. We can do our laundry together." Hilda clearly read the relief on June's face.

Hilda drove up and down several streets. She showed June the bank Frank used, the hair dresser she patronized, the library, her preferred drug store, Bockman's Department Store, and several other shops telling her which stores offered the best bargains or services. June knew she would not remember where all of them were, except the library. She planned to utilize it frequently. She was at a loss to know how she was going to spend her time.

Suddenly, she realized Hilda was asking her a question and June had not been listening. "I'm sorry, what did you say?"

"I said, Didn't you teach? This is our grade school. It's rather old but beautiful inside. We're very proud of it."

"Yes, I'm a teacher. I taught at a one room school for three years, grades one through eight. I had twenty-three students the first year, twenty my second year and eighteen last year. The older students kept quitting school to look for work to help their families."

"My! That must be a challenge, teaching all those grades."

"I loved it! I wonder if a teacher is needed here. It would be really something teaching just one grade. Can you show me the district office? I'd like to talk to them."

"Why Dear, you can't teach. You're married. The district would never hire you. And, I doubt if Frank would allow it."

"What? What's wrong with being married? And why would Frank mind? He's gone all week."

"I think you should just talk it over with Frank first. Oh, here's our church. I hope you will consider coming to church with us. Frank only comes on Easter and Christmas. Maybe if you start coming it will encourage Frank to come more regularly."

June only nodded. She did not acknowledge that her family were not regular church attendees, either. She was still miffed about what Hilda had said about her teaching.

Next, they drove to Ruth's home. It didn't look a whole lot better than Frank's house. It was a single-story clapboard house, in much need of paint. June thought, "I bet it at least has indoor plumbing."

"I hope you two become good friends. I didn't get along with my sister-in-law very well. We were so different." Hilda parked the car and both got out.

Hilda's grandson, Everett, was playing in

the front yard with a neighbor boy. Both mothers were sitting on porch chairs, each holding a baby. When Everett saw his grandma, he dropped the ball he was holding and ran to her. "Grandma, what did you bring me?"

"I brought you, your new aunt."

Everett stopped short and looked at June. "I don't like her. She looks like my teacher."

June started laughing so hard tears ran down her cheeks. Hilda was not so pleased. "Everett, you apologize. That was very rude."

"It's okay. Except for not liking me, I think it's a compliment." June turned to the boy and knelt to be on his level. "Everett, I am, a teacher. I hope you don't hold that against me. And I hope we become great friends."

"Sure," shouted Everett as he ran back to get his ball.

Ruth called to her mother, "Hi Mom, June. Come on up out of the sun. Peg, this is my new sister-in-law, June." June smiled at Peg. As Ruth made introductions, Hilda got chairs for herself and June.

Hilda and June sat down as Ruth continued, "I'm so glad you're here. We've been talking about Vacation Bible School. Peg offered to be the director again this year."

Peg looked at Hilda, "Are you going to help with snack time?"

"I have for the past fifteen or so years. Why stop now!"

"I'm glad to hear that. You do such a good job. Can I count on you to get your own helpers?"

Hilda nodded and smiled, "It'll probably be the same ones as last year. I just hope the church people are more generous bringing cookies than they were last year."

Ruth turned from watching Peg, and looked at her sister-in-law, "June, I know this is kind 'a sudden and you just arrived yesterday. But would you help me at VBS? I'm responsible for the six to seven-year-olds." Without taking a breath, Ruth hurriedly continued, "Except for story time, we only are required to lead the kids from one activity to the next. We'll have to be ready to assist the person in charge of the activity. We're on our own for story time. I know you used to teach school. I never even finished the tenth grade. I'm scared to death when I have to get up in front of people, even kids."

June just stared at Ruth. She had

never attended or worked in a Vacation Bible School in her life. She was not even sure what went on in one. Finally, she responded, "What exactly would I have to do?"

"Well, you know, we meet first in the sanctuary for announcements and some singing. Then we go to our separate rooms. Depending on the schedule we go to crafts, games, snacks, more singing and the Bible story time."

"So, what is the story time?"

The other three women gazed at June, finding it hard to believe she did not know what story time was. Peg came to the rescue. Picking up a VBS book she leafed through it, "Our Bible school theme this year is Old Testament Heroes. Each day a different Bible hero is covered. Some of them are David, Joseph, Joshua, and

Daniel. You just tell a simple story using the flannel graph. Then, there's a little activity for the children to do."

"I must confess, I don't know a lot about the Bible."

Peg continued, "So, neither do the kids. All you have to do is stay one day ahead of them. Let me give you the package for that age group. You can take it home and look it over. Let Ruth know. VBS is really lots of fun."

June sat holding the VBS package as Hilda drove to the local IGA® grocery store. She finally got up enough nerve to ask Hilda about VBS, "I don't know anything about VBS. How long does it last?"

"It's two weeks, Monday through Friday mornings, from 9:00 to 11:30."

"I don't even know what a flannelgraph is."

"It's a really good way to tell Bible stories. There is a large sheet of flannel with a scene painted on it. It's placed on a stand, like an easel. Then, as you tell a story you add flannel characters to the scene. The flannel cutouts will stick to the large flannel scene. I really think you should help out. It will be a great way to get acquainted with the other ladies in the church."

Chapter 5

All summer the weather had been hot and humid with very little breeze. June could not sleep beyond five o'clock. One day while in the basement helping Hilda with the laundry, June noticed an old end table. She wondered if Hilda would let her use it on her front porch to hold her coffee. Gathering up her courage she asked if she could have it.

Of course, Hilda said yes. Each morning she took a cup of cold coffee and a small plate holding a slice of bread with jam out to this table. She sat sipping the coffee and nibbling on the bread as she watched the day unfold. By now she recognized several of the train employees by the color of their caps and the neckerchiefs around their necks. They waved to her as their trains passed. The hobos riding the box cars would also wave. They all looked the same to June with lost looks on their faces and grubby looking clothes.

Hilda had been a jewel since June had arrived in Fairview. Patiently Hilda taught June to make a fire in the stove and how to control the oven temperature. She showed her how to clean the cookstove, a thoroughly repugnant job. It required using a broom, newspaper to rub parts of the stove with oil and applying a polish called stove black. Hilda told her stories of her early years of marriage and having to learn housekeeping duties. And if she had it to do over, she told her things she would still do and some she would not do.

Late one afternoon, to June's surprise, Hilda sat down in a kitchen chair. Looking at June she said, "June, sit down. I want to talk to you about something that is probably none of my business. But I'm going to say it anyway." June pulled out the second chair from under the table and sat. She looked at her mother-in-law with trepidation.

"Frank is only home on week-ends. Before you were married, when he was home, he ate his evening meals with us. I did all his laundry. He really doesn't understand how difficult it is for you living here. The depression has been hard. But Frank is not a pauper. I believe you can, and should, have a better place." Astonished, June stared at Hilda.

"I know you dislike, or should I say detest, living here. My talking like this has probably taken you by surprise. I also know Frank's obsession about Millicent's death. It is your decision how to handle these challenges. Please know I will, and have been praying for you and Frank. Well, I've said my piece. Now I must go home and fix Art's supper." They looked at each other and smiled!

June was in a quandary over Frank's constant talk of Millicent. She also despised the house. However, she was reluctant to say anything to Frank. She decided to bide her time.

June could now start a fire in the cookstove and make a somewhat decent meal. She hated the stove and everything else about this house. She looked at Baxter and said, "Hilda is right. She may have had to do such things in her life but that was forty years ago! Today there are modern conveniences. I shouldn't have to live like this. As she said we are not paupers."

She never heated up the stove except on week-ends when Frank was home. It had been such a hot summer. Today, it was only half past six and already the thermometer registered 86°. The thermometer was one given out to Frank's customers. It was about two feet long, painted bright yellow and showed product logos which R&R sold. It also listed information on how to contact them. June thought it was so crowded, one had to search to find the temperature. She really wanted a hot cup of coffee. Well, later she would walk to her in-laws house and get one.

Most days, June walked into town. She now had a library card and knew many of the people in town. Today was going to be different. She was determined to go to the school district office to ask the superintendent about a teaching job. She did not mention this to Frank. Maybe if she had a position first, he would not be as likely to object.

Before she left for town, she needed to get ready for Vacation Bible School which started next Monday. The church always scheduled Bible School the first two weeks in August. How she dreaded the thought! "Why did I agree to help? What do I know about the Bible? Just stay one day ahead of the kids. HUH!"

June had found a Bible in one of the Hoosier cupboard's drawers. She did not think it had been read much. The story for the first day of VBS was titled "From Slave to Ruler", and was about Joseph. To her surprise the story was not the Christmas story about Mary, her husband, Joseph, and the baby Jesus. This was a different Joseph. As she read the Bible references, she was glad the story was in Genesis, the first book of the Bible. That was easy to fine. She became more and more absorbed in the astonishing story, reading beyond the given verses.

Joseph had been sold into slavery by his own brothers. He had been mistreated and lied about. But he always remained faithful to God. She never knew such stories were in the Bible. This was amazing!

June cut out the flannel figures before stopping. It was almost noon. She could not believe how long she had been reading and working. Her stomach was telling her what time it was. After eating a peanut butter sandwich and a couple of cookies, she cleaned up, fixed her hair and put on her blue cotton dress, her white mules and a white broad brimmed hat. It was the coolest ensemble she had. A pair of white gloves rested on the dresser. June knew she should wear them, but oh, it was so hot! She put them in her purse thinking she could slip them on later.

June knew the location of the district school office. On her way there, she detoured over two blocks to Fir Street. She had walked down Fir Street several times. In the middle of the block was a small house made of fieldstone. The roof was cedar shingles. It was not very big and reminded her of a fairy tale cottage. The first time she happened upon the house her heart stopped. In the front yard, attached to a pole, pounded into the ground, was a sign that read, "For Sale"!

The sign was still there as June stood on

the sidewalk in front of the house dreaming about owning it. She had not noticed a lady deadheading flowers along the connecting fence. "Good afternoon. You're Frank Grimes's new wife, aren't you?" Startled, June looked at her. "My name's Mabel Cunningham." June continued to stare as Mabel walked to the edge of her lot extending her right hand.

June walked to the fence and offered her hand, "I'm sorry. Yes, my name's June. It's nice to meet you."

"I take it you like the house. I've seen you here a couple of times."

"Yes, I do. Can you tell me about it?"

Mabel opened the white picket fence gate and beckoned June in. "Come on in, out of the sun. We can sit on the porch. Would you like a glass of lemonade? I was about to have one brought to me."

June followed Mabel to the porch. A large bur oak tree gave cooling shade. Sitting on a very ornate metal table was a small bell. Mabel picked up the bell and gave it a slight tingle. "Let's sit down." No sooner had she said this when a girl who looked to be in her early teens opened the screen door and came over to the ladies. "Dorothea, please, get us some lemonade. Be sure to put more ice in it than you did last time. And, bring some of those cookies I showed you how to make yesterday."

Dorothea smiled and returned to the house, letting the screen door bang. "Oh, that girl! If I've told her once, I've told her a hundred times, not to let the door bang. I only took her on because my cousin is friends with her mother and said the family is in such dire straits."

"That is very nice of you Mrs. Cunningham. What can you tell me about the house?"

"Well, it's like so many other houses these days. The family, their name was Sherman, owned the place. Bill Sherman lost his job in '31'. After that he worked at any job he could find trying to keep his family fed and the bills paid."

Just then Dorothea returned with a tray holding the lemonade and a plate of Russian tea cakes. She plunked the tray on the table causing some of the lemonade to splash on the cakes. Mrs. Cunningham admonished Dorothea, who turned on her heels without saying a word. She let the screen door bang as she returned to the house.

Mabel sat looking at the screen door exasperated. Shaking her head, she turned back to the table and poured two glasses of lemonade before continuing her story. "Now where was I? Oh yes, one night Barney, that's my husband, and I heard quite a commotion next door. We watched out our bedroom window as the Shermans packed up their Ford with all it could hold, put the sleeping kids in the back seat, on top of the suitcases, and drove off. Never saw them again."

"Does the bank hold the mortgage on the house?"

"No, it's the Fairview Savings and Loan. Why, are you thinking of buying it? It's been empty three years now. A boy comes by to mow, but as you've seen, not often enough. Barney has taken it upon himself to mow it occasionally when the grass gets really long. If I weren't so old, and it wasn't so hot, I'd go pull the weeds from the flowers. It used to be a really pretty place. And it can be again. Do you think you and Frank might buy it?"

"No, not really. I just like looking at it."

"You could probably get it at a good price. It's haunted."

"Haunted!"

"Yes, or so everyone says. Of course, no one has ever seen a ghost".

"Then why do people say it's haunted?"

"Every once in a while, you can hear music being played on a guitar. The original owner, a man named Ezekiel Howard, was playing his guitar the night he died. Some say his ghost returns on the date of his death to serenade folks. Of course, Lucille, that's Mrs. Sherman, said she heard the music more than once a year."

"I don't believe in ghosts. There must be some logical reason why music can be heard. Oh, look at the time. Mrs. Cunningham, I must get going. I want to thank you so much for the interesting conversation and the lemonade. It was really good," June lied. It was very sour but maybe Mabel liked it that way.

June left thinking about the house. "How I would love to see the inside. "Does it have two bedrooms or three? What does the kitchen look like? There is a brick chimney going up the outside. Maybe the living room has a fireplace. And indoor plumbing! Phooey, about the ghost! Ghost, indeed!"

By the time June walked to the school office she was drenched in sweat. Stopping at the ladies' restroom, she attempted to make herself more presentable. First, she removed her hat then splashed cold water on her face and applied a light coating of lipstick. Rummaging in her purse, she found a comb and did the best she could to make her hair look presentable. She took the white gloves out of her purse and put them on. Finally, she pinned the hat back on. She was glad it was broad brimmed as it covered most of her clammy hair.

The office was one of two on the third floor of the First Bank of Fairview. To greet June, an older lady wearing a severe black dress with long sleeves and a high collar looked up from a neatly organized desk. "May I help you?"

"Yes, thank you. My name is June Grimes. I'm an experienced teacher and would like to apply for a position."

"Aren't you Frank Grimes's new wife?"

"Yes, that's right."

"We don't hire married women."

June stood looking down at this woman, not knowing what to say. Finally, she formed her words very carefully. "May I please, see the superintendent?"

"I just told you. We don't hire married women."

"May I, please, see the superintendent?"

The secretary sighed, got up from her desk and knocked on the superintendent's door, opened it and entered. She was gone only a few seconds. The door opened and June was ushered in.

June stepped into a dark, wood-paneled room. The floor was covered partially with a beautiful red rug. The room was very cool. She thought it must be air cooled somehow. "Mr. Neuman this is Mrs. Grimes." The secretary said her name slowly, emphasizing the Mrs. as she closed the door.

"Please sit down, Mrs. Grimes. So, you want a teaching job? I'm surprised you got past Miss Evans. She can be quite formidable. However, we don't hire married teachers."

June sat primly at the edge of her chair, "Why? What's wrong with marriage? Aren't all the mothers of the children married?"

"That's just it. A married woman's place is in the home, caring for her children."

"I don't have any children. I live in a very small house. It takes about thirty minutes to clean."

"Yes, but in no time at all, you will be a

mother with children, and have to quit. We can't have women 'in the family way' in front of the children. It's hard to tell what that might lead to!"

"Well, I bet most of the children have younger siblings. And if they have pets, they have babies. How many of your students live on farms?"

Mr. Neuman sighed, rested his left elbow on the desk and leaned his cheek into his curled hand. He stared at June. June thought he was going to tell her to leave. To her surprise he said, "Would you be interested in substituting?"

June's countenance lit up with a smile, "Yes!"

Mr. Neuman opened a desk drawer and pulled out a paper, "Now, I can't promise anything for sure. This will have to go before the board of directors. They may shoot it down. But we are always short of substitute teachers. Fill this out and give it to Miss Evans. Good luck"

June completed the form before leaving the building. She handed it to Miss Evans who actually grumbled something to June. June did not care. She left with a spring in her step.

That week-end June told Frank about submitting her request to substitute teach. Frank did not say anything. He was sure no one would hire a married woman. The only teachers he had ever had were single or widowed or in high school, men.

 **Chapter 6**

June surprisingly enjoyed Vacation Bible School. She thought, "Am I learning more than the children? Who knew all these wonderful stories: like Daniel in the lion's den, the three men in the furnace and Queen Esther were in the Bible?" Her favorite was still Joseph. She read about him over and over.

All the time she was learning children's Bible stories, God was speaking to her heart. Traditionally, the pastor gave a salvation talk to the children during the story time on the second Thursday. He would invite all the children, who wanted to give their hearts to Jesus and follow Him, to come forward to the altar and pray. The leaders were expected to be at the altar to help the children. June was petrified.

Her heart was heavy. How could she help the children when she needed to ask forgiveness and accept Jesus as her Savior? She thought about not coming Thursday. She could call Ruth, telling her she was sick and would not be there. She could not do that. Ruth needed her help. Before leaving the church on Wednesday, she asked Pastor Johnson if they could talk. She confessed her dilemma.

Pastor Johnson graciously asked June, "Do you want to accept Jesus as your Savior?"

"Yes, I do. For the past two weeks I've been reading these Bible stories. God has spoken to me as I hope He has to the children. I need the Savior. But I really don't know what to do."

"June, it's as easy as ABC. A, accept the fact you're a sinner." Pastor Johnson opened his Bible, "The apostle Paul wrote in Romans 3:23, 'For all have sinned and come short of the glory of God'." He pointed out the verse, as he read it to her. "The B stands for believe Jesus died for your sins. Romans 5:8 tells us, 'But God commendeth his love toward us, in that, while we were yet sinners, Christ died for us.' Lastly, C, you need to confess your sins, receiving Jesus as your Savior and live for Him." The pastor gave the Bible to June. "Here, you read Romans 10:9."

With a little catch in her throat, June read, "'That if thou shalt confess with thy mouth the Lord Jesus, and shalt believe in thine heart that God hath raised him from the dead, thou shalt be saved.'" June continued to hold the Bible, looking down at it. Blinking back tears, she handed the Bible to Pastor Johnson.

"Would you like to pray?" June nodded, folded her hands in her lap and bowed her head.

Pastor Johnson bowed his head and said, "Say these words after me. Dear Heavenly Father, I know I'm a sinner."

Quietly June repeated Pastor Johnson's words, "Dear heavenly Father, I know I'm a sinner."

The pastor continued, "I believe your Son, Jesus, came to earth, suffered and died on the cross for my sins."

June again restated his words.

Finally, Pastor Johnson said, "I confess my

sins and ask Jesus to come into my heart. Please help me to live for You. Amen."

After again following Pastor Johnson's words, June opened her teary eyes and removed her glasses. She nervously took out her handkerchief from her purse and cleaned them. At last, June asked, "Is that it?"

"If by faith, you truly believe what you said, then yes, you are a new person in Christ. Welcome to the family of God."

"What about that part you said about living for Jesus?"

"Although salvation cannot be earned, true faith and righteous works go hand in hand. God wants us to live in such a way that our lives show we have repented. Just as in marriage, out of love, you desire to please your partner, so it is with loving God.

"We do not do good deeds so God will love us. He already loves us. However, loving God should make us want to do good and avoid evil. As you grow in Christ, He may show you things in your life that would be better for you not to do. For example, as a teen-ager, my wife was addicted to roller skating. She went to the roller rink every chance she had. She said that she would even skip school to go skating. Sometimes she stole money from her mother's purse or her sister's piggy bank to get money to go. One day God spoke to her asking what she loved more, her skates or Him. The only way she could control her desire was to stop going completely. Now there is nothing wrong with skating. The church has skating parties for the teens once a month. And on occasion I will take my children to the roller ring. Mrs. Johnson stays home."

June looked at the pastor astonished, "Oh, my!"

Pastor Johnson continued, "God will let you know if there is anything in your life that will be detrimental to your spiritual walk. Paul had something to say in a letter to the Philippians. Let's look at Philippians 2:12." As he said this he turned to the passage and handed the Bible to June. "Here, you read what it says."

Pensively, June accepted the Bible once again, "Wherefore, my beloved, as ye have always obeyed, not as in my presence only, but now much more in my absence, work out your own salvation with fear and trembling." She handed the Bible back to Rev. Johnson looking at him questioningly.

"You are probably wondering about what 'fear and trembling' means. In our present way of speaking those words would be reverent and sensitive to God's guiding.

"You may find the book of James thought-provoking. It is near the back of your Bible. He has some interesting things to say about doing good. Most importantly, make prayer and reading your Bible a daily habit. God will show you how to live a spiritual life."

June felt a lightness in her heart as she walked home. She knew a burden had been lifted from her soul. She decided to stop at her in-laws to tell them about what she had done.

June did not bother to knock. As she entered the back door Hilda was holding the refrigerator door open and looking inside. "Hello June. Come on in. I'm just about to fix myself some lunch. Art is off doing something. I don't know what.

He said he wouldn't be home for lunch. Sit down and join me." June was rather relieved that her father-in-law was not at home. It seemed easier to talk to Hilda alone.

"Thanks Hilda. I will stay, but first I want to tell you something."

"You're not pregnant, are you?"

June smiled, "No Hilda, not yet."

"Please forgive me. I shouldn't be prying like that. What is it you want to tell me?"

"I had a meeting with Pastor Johnson after VBS this morning. I accepted Jesus as my Savior. I'm a new Christian."

Hilda came over to June, giving her a big hug. "June, that is wonderful, just wonderful. I've been praying for you and Frank every day. Let's have a celebration," she said as she put items back in the refrigerator. "We'll go out to the 'Painted Porch' for lunch."

"The what?"

"The 'Painted Porch'. It's an old farm house just north of town. Art calls it a foo-foo place, just for ladies. He'd never go there. You'll love it."

June gasped as Hilda guided her car down a winding gravel road through a grove of oak trees to an old two-story farm house. It appeared to have been recently painted a pleasing pale yellow. The trim around the windows was painted a darker sunflower yellow. The front wall of the house enclosed by the porch was mint green. Climbing yellow roses trailed around the railings and porch pillars which were painted raspberry pink. Several cars were parked in a gravel parking area.

Hilda parked the car and the two walked towards the porch. June noticed the navy-blue scuffed porch floor. "I can see why this is called 'The Painted Porch'. How did you ever find this place?"

"Well, the owners, are Stella Getz and her sister Ella Stover. Stella has lived here all her life with her parents. I went to school with Ella. When the sisters' father died, the mother needed a way to make money. She put up a sign on the road and started fixing meals people could buy and carry home with them.

"After the mother died, there was some insurance money. The sisters used it to improve the place and opened a lunch time restaurant. It was closed for about three years during the worst of the hard times. They've been open again for the last couple of years."

A rough looking young man, who appeared to be in his early twenties, was working in a lovely flower garden. He stood up as the two ladies passed. June could feel his eyes on her. It caused her to shiver. Hilda noticed June tensing up as they walked by, "Don't worry about him June. That's Ella's son, Eddie. He's a little strange. He doesn't like to be around people."

"Does he stare at everyone?"

"That I couldn't say. Ella's husband was killed in the Great War. She and her three kids moved back here with Stella and their parents. Her oldest daughter, Mildred is now the manager of the place. She lives in town. The other girl is married and lives in the west some place. Eddie still lives here with his mom and aunt. He's mentally slow and a loner."

June understood why Art called the

restaurant a foo-foo place. The entrance hall was painted robin's egg blue. She thought the garishly wallpapered room to her left must have at one time been the main parlor. The bright purple and yellow wallpaper was worse than the wallpaper in her own living room. She did not believe it could have been possible.

The main parlor had several tables scattered about. Each table was covered with a different type of tablecloth. One was red and white checked. A couple were lace. Another was a wild print. No two-place settings were the same. Some of the China dishes looked to be antique.

The only patrons were women and girls. One table accommodated a group of four little girls and their mothers celebrating a birthday. Each girl was wearing beautiful lace and bow covered pastel dresses. On a side table were several gifts wrapped in bright tissue with lovely ribbons. Next to the gifts was a cake that looked to have more candied flowers and icing than cake.

Near the back, sat four very old ladies dressed to the nines. Their garments had been quite stylish at the turn of the century. The older ladies saw Hilda, waved, and spoke to her.

Hilda was talking to one of the ladies when a young hostess approached to show June and her mother-in-law to a room across the hall. It looked like it could have once been a second parlor. This room was more pleasing than the first parlor. It was decorated with wallpaper of thin green, blue and pink stripes. Several heads leaned together as the two were shown to their table. Once Hilda and June were seated, Hilda smiled at June, "Most likely they're gossiping about your being the new Mrs. Frank Grimes. There isn't much that goes on around this town that everyone sooner or later doesn't find out about". June looked around the room and smiled at each table.

A very pretty waitress dressed in an antique looking maid's uniform took their order. While they waited June asked, "What about Stella? Didn't she ever get married?"

"Her story is a sad one. Stella was engaged to a really handsome man by the name of Charlie Jones. She was the envy of all of us girls. I was actually to be one of her bride's maids. Oh, was my dress ever pretty, and expensive! My dad had a fit at the cost. Then just two days before the wedding, Charlie came to Stella and said he didn't want to marry her.

"I'm not sure Stella ever got over the

disappointment. She was shattered. Just shattered!"

"Did you ever hear why this Charlie fellow backed out?"

"Some years later Art and I met Charlie's brother. We got to talking and Art not being one to mince words, asked him right out why Charlie broke the engagement. He said Charlie had told him, he couldn't imagine waking up every morning for the rest of his life, listening to Stella's gravelly voice."

"Stella's voice?"

"Yes. If she has a chance, she will most likely come out of the kitchen to say hello. She's the main cook, and a very good one. However, she doesn't have a very pleasant voice. But you'd think Charlie could have decided that before asking her to marry him."

"I think it's terrible. No one is perfect. Surely, she has many good qualities that attracted him to her."

"I hope you get to meet her. She is one of the kindest and sweetest persons that ever-walked God's green earth.

"June, by-the-way, there is something I have been wanting to talk to you about." June looked at her mother-in-law with alarm. What could it be? Was there some shortcoming, Hilda did not like about her?

"I felt really bad we couldn't come to your wedding and meet your folks. Art just didn't feel he could drive that far. He was still recovering from his injuries from the accident at work. He encouraged me to go by train. But I felt he really needed me at home. I hope you and your folks don't hold it against us."

June reached across the table to take Hilda's hand. "Of course, we don't. We understood. Times are difficult. There will be time later for you and my parents to meet. Mother is going to send me the pictures of the wedding as soon as they're ready. She's getting a large one of Frank and me, just for you."

"That is so nice. Would you tell me a little about yourself? Frank isn't one to share much."

June thought to herself before answering her mother-in-law, "Boy, that sure is the truth!" Out loud June said, "There isn't really a lot to tell. My dad's family came to America several generations ago from England. The men have been quite successful in business. My mom is mostly Irish.

"I was the first to graduate from college on

my mother's side of the family. My brother, Carl, will be a junior in college this fall. And my younger brother, Martin, is a senior in high school. And I am a brand-new child in God's family!"

As June was telling this the waitress brought their lunch. Conversation lessened as both enjoyed a foo-foo lunch of cold fruit soup, curried macaroni and herring salad, rye bread, rhubarb compote, spritz ring cookies and very strong coffee. June would not be eating much supper tonight.

 # Chapter 7

Frank continued to talk about Millicent. To hear him, one would think she had been a saint. June prayed and prayed about how to handle the situation. She went to Pastor Johnson one day to seek his counsel. She began to cry as she related the situation.

Pastor Johnson seemed to understand. "June, to save your marriage, you must talk to Frank about your feelings. If you don't tell him, he will never understand how you feel. We men are not like women, we don't pick up on nuances. We have to be told point blank."

"I don't want to hurt him."

"Do you want to go on in your marriage like this?"

"No, of course not."

"I think Frank is hurting also. Possibly by bringing out your feelings, it will help him examine his rationale and open up to you."

By Friday June had decided to really talk to Frank about Millicent and how it was destroying their marriage. All day she busied herself in anticipation. He was late arriving. She figured he had stopped at the cemetery.

The first thing Frank noticed, walking into the front room, was Millicent's picture missing. "June?"

"In the kitchen, Darling."

Frank did not say hello or give June a

kiss. "Millicent's picture's gone. What's happened to it?"

June ignored his question. "Supper's ready. We'll talk after eating. Let's go sit on the back porch, it's a little cooler. Bring chairs with you."

Frank looked at June suspiciously as he picked up two chairs and carried them to the porch. June carried out two plates of food. She had found a card table in an outbuilding, had washed it and was using it on the back porch. June bowed her head in prayer. Silently she asked God for guidance. Without saying anything, both began to eat.

"This meatloaf is good, but not as good as Millicent used to make. She really knew how to work a kitchen."

June put down her fork and looked at

Frank. Her appetite was gone. Frank continued to eat unmindful of June.

"I put it in the hope chest."

"What?"

"I said, I put Millicent's picture in the hope chest."

"Why?"

June looked intently into Frank's soft brown eyes, clinched her teeth and sighed. "When you came home, the first thing you did, was look for Millicent's picture."

"Yeah, so what?"

"Millicent is your dead wife. I am your living wife." Frank started to say something. June held up her hand to stop him. "Please let me continue.

"I will admit, I have never experienced the

death of someone as close as a spouse. I've only had a grandfather and a cousin die. So, I can't say that I fully understand your sorrow.

"However, there is a shadow standing between us. That shadow is Millicent. I know I can't cook very well. I don't like large garish flowers on the walls. Or many other things Millicent evidently liked and did well. I like to read. I enjoy going places, not staying at home day after day. And I resent your trying to remake me into a dead woman. I feel like I'm in an adulterous affair.

"You're going to have to make a decision." June hurriedly continued, "You must decide if you want to live with the shadow of a dead wife or with a living wife. This marriage will not survive with your heart in two worlds. I love you so very much; but a dead woman's shadow is blocking your love for me."

Frank looked at his wife, a fork-full of meatloaf midway to his mouth. He set the fork on his plate. June noted a teary mist in his eyes. She loved this man so very much and oh, how she wanted their marriage to thrive.

Frank looked down at his plate and spoke softly, "I know you're right June. I've seen the hurt in your eyes when I talk about Millicent. I know it's wrong. It's…just… that I have such guilt and shame about her death."

"Why?"

Frank looked up into those lovely blue eyes, "It's my fault she died. She only wanted a telephone. I told her it wasn't necessary. We had Baxter to protect her. She was only eighteen and I thought she would be on the phone all day talking to her girlfriends. It never entered my mind she would get sick and need to call for help." He gazed at June, "I guess when I talk about her it lessens my guilt."

"Tell me about her death."

"It was winter. There had been a really terrible storm. All the roads were closed. I didn't get home until late on Saturday. The house was freezing because the fire in the stove was out.

"At first, I figured Millicent must have gone to her folks or maybe a friend's house. Then I looked in the bedroom. She was on the bed all huddled up under all the blankets we had. I went to wake her but she was cold and stiff. The doctor said by the time I found her; she had been dead two days. He did an autopsy. Her appendix had burst. She must have been in terrible agony before she died."

"I'm really sorry, Frank."

"She wasn't the perfect wife I've made her out to be. She was barely seventeen when we married. She was a spoilt, selfish girl. She wasn't a good cook. She only went to my mom's house once to bake bread. She said her mom told her, she would teach her anything she needed to know and not to go to a stranger's house. Making her into this faultless person somehow eased my sorrow. But, I did it at your expense and it was so, so wrong."

June got up and knelt beside Frank taking his hands, "Let me tell you about my mother. When she was a young girl, it was her and her younger sister's job to clean the soot off the glass chimneys of the kerosene lamps each morning. One day her little sister spilt some kerosene on her dress. My mom took a match and was teasing her, saying she wondered how close she could get the match to the dress without catching it on fire. Suddenly, the dress burst into flames. My mom's sister burned to death.

"My mom has had to deal with that tragedy the rest of her life. She only talked to me about it one time. She said she always felt her mom, my grandmother, never liked her after that because of causing her sister's death.

"I asked her how she was able to go on and live a normal life. Many years she suffered with depression and felt no one loved her. At the age of fifteen, she tried to kill herself. The nurse took time to talk to her. Mom said the nurse was very kind and told her there was nothing she could do to change what had happened. She encouraged Mom to ask Jesus to take her pain away and give her peace. The nurse prayed, then she had my mom pray. Mom said she told God she was sorry for what had happened and asked Him for peace for herself and for her parents.

"The nurse urged Mom to talk to her parents about the accident. After she left the hospital, she did bring up the incident with her parents. At first my grandma wouldn't talk about it. Finally, my grandma opened up and took my mom in her arms and said she knew it was just a foolish mistake of a youngster. All those years she had felt guilty for leaving the two girls alone unsupervised. Grandma told my mom she was sorry for treating her so poorly.

"My mom says there are still times when

depression threatens to overwhelm her. But she remembers the day in the hospital, she gave the pain to Jesus and is comforted.

"Frank, give your grief and regret to Jesus. Ask Him to help you. I believe He will."

"I'm not sure I believe in all that stuff. I just need to think before I say something. I'll try to be a better husband. I do love you June. Please don't leave me."

"I'll not leave you. I love you and married you for better or for worse, in sickness and in health and for richer or for poorer, until death us do part. I will pray for you, though. Let me pray for you right now."

"Sure, why not!"

June continued to hold Frank's hand. "Dear Heavenly Father, we come to you, first, to thank you for the gift of Jesus, who came as a man to die on the cross to save us. I thank you for the comfort you can give if we only ask. I thank you for the comfort you have given my mom and ask you to open Frank's eyes to the peace that can be his. In the blessed name of Jesus, Amen."

"That was real nice June. Can we finish eating now?"

Chapter 8

June had started going to the Wednesday night prayer meetings at the church. She enjoyed these informal services. Pastor Johnson would ask if there was anyone who desired to give a testimony of how God was working in his or her life. June had yet to stand up and say anything, but she enjoyed hearing others speak.

Normally June's in-laws attended the services and drove her home afterwards. This Wednesday, however, Art was not feeling well and they had stayed home. After the meeting a couple of people offered to drive June home. She decided there was still enough light to safely walk home.

June was enjoying the cool breeze as she strolled slowly home. She had not realized just how dark it had gotten until she passed the Samson house. It was the last residence before a large open field, then her house. As June neared her home, she could just barely see something in the front yard next to the walk. Slowly she approached the object. "Baxter! What's the matter? Are you sick?" She started to kneel next to the dog when, out of the corner of her eye, she saw a dark shape coming towards her. An instinct told her to run.

She left Baxter, and retreated across the open field running as fast as she ever had in her whole life. Reaching the Samson's backyard, she rounded the garage. Two galvanized steel trash cans stood next to the closed garage door. Darting between the two cans she squatted making herself as small as possible. She was wearing a light blue print dress and a small white hat. She looked up at the full moon and realized there was no way the stranger would not discover her hiding place. "Oh God", she prayed, "please help me." Just as she heard footsteps on the gravel driveway, a dark cloud glided over the moon. All was dark. The man stood in the middle of the driveway looking all around. He looked directly at the two trash cans. June held her breath. She heard the man curse as he slowly turned and walked back the way he had come.

June continued crouching until she could no longer remain in the uncomfortable position. Slowly standing up, she leaned against the garage wall and watched as the cloud sailed on past the moon. She made a dash for the Samson's back door and began to bang loudly, "Help me, please help me!" Over and over, she shouted. Finally, the door opened.

"Why, Mrs. Grimes! Come in. What's the matter? Are you okay?" June fell unceremoniously into Mr. Samson's arms and started crying hysterically. Wearing a wrapper and a hair net over curlers, Mrs. Samson came into the room. Mr. Samson was only too glad to hand off June to her. Rita Samson led June to a chair.

"Joe, get Mrs. Grimes a glass of water." Looking at June she asked, "June, do you want us to call the police?" June bobbed her head.

Soon two policemen arrived, followed minutes later by Frank's parents. June leapt into her mother-in-law's arms starting to cry again. "There, there, Darling. Sit back down. Tell us what happened."

Still holding on to Hilda, June related the incident ending with, "I think Baxter is dead. I can't go back to that house. I'm so scared!"

"You don't have to, Dear. You can come and stay with us."

A police officer interrupted this exchange. "Mrs. Grimes, did you get a look at the man?"

"No, officer, not really. I only got a glimpse out of the corner of my eye of him coming at me. When I was hiding by the garage a cloud covered the moon and I just saw him standing in the driveway. He had on a hat that shadowed his face." June started reliving the scene over again and began to shake and hiccup.

"Really, Jake! June has been through enough right now. We're taking her home. Come by tomorrow if you must talk to her." This was spoken by Art, June's father-in-law. Hilda was surprised and pleased by this. Art seldom stood up to anyone.

Once home Hilda gave her one of her night gowns and helped June into a bed in the spare room. She handed June a pill, "Take this. It will calm you and help you sleep."

June swallowed the pill, "Please stay with me. I don't want to be alone." Hilda sat down in a near-by rocking chair and smiled.

"Good morning, Darling." June felt a soft kiss on her cheek. She opened her eyes to a bright sunny day. "I wondered if you were going to sleep the day away."

"Frank! Oh, Frank." June raised herself

up and hugged Frank. "When did you get here? How did you know?"

"Dad called me at the hotel where I was staying. I got here about three this morning. Are you all right?"

"I have a bit of a headache and feel kind of dull."

Frank gave a gentle chuckle, "You most likely have a hangover from the pill Mom gave you. She's a great one for medicating."

Frank started to sit down in the rocking chair, but June would not let him go. "Frank, I was so scared. The man killed Baxter."

"Hush now. I'm so sorry this all happened to you. The good news is, Baxter is not dead. He was still alive when Michael, that's one of the policemen, found him.

He took him to the vet, Doc Nelson's on Chalmers Street. The vet said he's going to be okay."

"Thank God. Frank, I'm really scared. Please, I don't want to live out there anymore. Please, please, can't we move into town? I don't want to be alone."

"Oh, Darling, I'm sorry for being such a poor excuse for a husband. I should have asked you about moving when we first got married. I knew the minute you saw the house you didn't like it. I know you are used to much nicer things."

"It's not that, exactly. It's just so lonely out there and scary."

"You get dressed and come down to breakfast or maybe by now we should call it lunch! While I'm waiting for you, I'll give my friend, Clyde Everard, a call. He and his dad own the Everard Realty."

June lay in bed a few minutes longer, after Frank left the room to call his friend. She lifted a prayer to God, "Thank you, Lord, for watching over me last night. I know you caused the cloud to hide the moon. Thank you. And thank you for Baxter being okay. You also know how I would love to see the inside of the stone house. If it would please you, please, let it happen."

Later in the afternoon, June and Frank walked to the Everard Realty. It was a beautiful fall day. Hilda had washed the clothes June had worn the day before. June had heard such awful stories, kidding or not, about mothers-in-law. She felt blessed to have such a good one.

Clyde Everard had several pages describing homes for sale scattered about his desk.

June spied the stone house description immediately. She picked up the paper. "I've seen this one on my walks about town. Can we view it?"

Frank bent over June's shoulder, "That's the haunted house."

June turned and looked at Frank, "You don't really believe in ghosts and haunted houses, do you?"

"Well, I guess not. But, why this particular house?"

June explained about her walks about town. "I really like the looks of this house. Please, let's look at it."

Clyde drove the couple to the Fir Street location in his 1938, Fair Haven Blue Cadillac. It seemed to June, who was sitting in the back seat, he was taking an overly long route. She felt uncomfortable as she noticed people stopping and watching as they passed. Frank and Clyde had a running discussion about high school football games which left June out of the conversation.

The trio finally arrived at the house. June saw Mrs. Cunningham watching them and waved to her. June already knew the porch wrapped around the front and side of the house. There was a side door at the end of the porch which June suspected opened to the kitchen.

Clyde unlocked the front door and ushered the couple in. The door opened onto the living room with honey colored hardwood flooring. The inside of the house was everything June had imagined it to be. There was a red brick fireplace on the west wall. On either side of the fireplace were maple bookcases. The wood floor continued through a wide arched opening into the dining room. French doors opened off the dining room onto a small stone terrace.

To the right of the dining room was a spacious kitchen. The first thing June noticed was a Detroit Jewel Gas Stove. It had four burners, a broiler, an oven, a warming drawer, and a storage bin.

"Frank! Look at this stove! It can't be more than five or six years old. The oven even has a gauge to control the temperature! And look at this refrigerator. It's almost new." The refrigerator was an unusual General Electric double door model. The refrigeration compressor unit sat on top of the case. "It's so big, I won't have to go to the store every day."

"Yes, Mrs. Grimes, those are quality appliances. The Shermans were doing okay before the crash. But, like too many people they had over extended themselves. They lost it all".

Frank looked at Clyde, "Where do these two doors lead to?"

"Behind this door is a small pantry," he answered him as he opened the door. "The other one goes to the basement. Want to see it?"

Frank looked at June. "Are you interested in going down?"

"Not right now. I take it this third door opens onto the side porch?" As June said this, she opened the door. She could imagine herself taking a cup of coffee and sitting out on the porch. She could even invite Mrs. Cunningham over to join her. Turning to Clyde she asked, "Can we see the bedrooms?"

Leading off the east side of the living room was an alcove. On either side of the alcove were doors leading to two large bedrooms. The front bedroom had a window looking out to the front yard and one adjacent to the Cunningham's driveway. It was papered in a pleasing soft gray with tiny blue and white flowers. The floor was the same honey colored hardwood as the living and dining rooms.

The second bedroom was a bit smaller. It also had a hardwood floor and two windows. They overlooked the driveway and the backyard. The walls were papered with a 19th century toile hunting scene in shades of cream and green. The hunters were all wearing red clothing. "Wow! That's really some wallpaper. I bet you'll have that changed real quick," Frank looked at June and smiled.

Straight in from the alcove was a bathroom. White 3x6 glazed ceramic tile covered the wall to about half way up. It was capped with pencil bullnose tile. The upper half of the walls were papered with green ferns on a white background. Hexagonal white and black glazed tile covered the floor. A Windsor sink with an over-sized bowl sat impressively along one side. At the end of the room was a bathtub. "Look, Frank! A tub with a shower! Can you believe it?" She also observed the commode. Oh, this was the house she wanted!

Once back at the real estate office Frank put down earnest money on the house. Then Frank and June holding hands, walked back to the elder Grimes's home.

"June, there is something I'm going to tell you which I know you'll like."

June stopped and turned to look at her husband. "What would that be?"

"Do you remember meeting my manager, Old Man Forester?"

"Yes. I remember he looked old enough to have known Moses." Both gave a chuckle.

"Well, he's finally retiring and I've been offered the job of district manager!"

"Does that mean you won't be traveling so much? You'll be home at night?"

"Yes! I'll be home every night. I hope you can stand me, underfoot all the time." June wanted to hug her husband, but knew propriety did not allow such a show of affection in public. She just beamed with happiness.

"The job also comes with a hefty raise.

Which means we don't need to sell the other place."

"Why do you want to keep that place? What good is it?" June feared Frank's wanting to keep the old house had something to do with Millicent's memory.

"I believe in the not-too-distant future that property is going to be very valuable. It's right across the street from the tracks and the town will be growing. Someday we'll get a better price for it than we would right now."

 **Chapter 9**

The happy couple moved into the stone house late in October. Several men from the church offered to help them move. Frank, ever cynical, thought they were volunteering only to make him feel guilty about not going to church. There really wasn't much the Grimes had to move. Along with the new bedroom set, they also moved the kitchen table, chairs, and Hoosier cupboard. June hoped it wouldn't be long before they could buy a new dining room set. Frank's parents arrived with the boxes of wedding presents they had been storing. June was glad to see them. She yearned to have a reason to use the china and silver.

Before moving, Frank had a bonfire and burned his old living room couch and chair. He also took the cedar chest with its contents over to Millicent's mother explaining to June, "All of the stuff in it was Millicent's. Maybe her mother will get some comfort out of the things." This also included the beautiful picture of Millicent.

From Duly's Furniture Store, the couple purchased a new living room set, a French style high back tufted winged sofa and two matching chairs. One of the chairs was a rocker. Frank chose the velvet fabric: cigar brown with thin pale gold stripes. June didn't like the name but thought it looked modern.

Two end tables and a coffee table arrived with the living room suite. A note attached to the coffee table stated it was a house warming gift from the senior Grimes.

Duke and Ruth stopped by later that evening. They presented June and Frank with a floor lamp and matching table lamp. It wasn't the style June would have chosen. She graciously accepted the gifts.

Three days later a van pulled into the driveway. The driver unloaded two large boxes. June unwrapped them and discovered they were two pieces of art from her parents. The larger of the two was by Paul E. Harney. It was an Autumn landscape with two women walking beside a river. It would look grand hanging over the sofa. The smaller very unusual one was by Rosa Bonheur. Three shepherds were rowing a boat load of sheep across a river. June had grown up loving both pictures. The Harney had hung in her mother's bedroom. The Bonheur painting was from her father's study. June's heart swelled with gratitude and love as she viewed the gifts.

The couple had lived in the house about two weeks. The wind had been blowing all afternoon with intermittent showers. About 2 a.m. June was awakened by the sound like the strumming of a guitar. She grabbed Frank's arm. "Frank, do you hear the music?"

Frank turned over, "Hear what?"

"The guitar. Don't you hear it?"

"No, I don't hear anything. Go back to sleep."

After a few minutes the sound stopped. June lay still. She decided in the morning, she was going to find out the source of the music.

The next morning was wash day. The rain had stopped but there was still a stiff breeze. Frank had left for work early to go with a new hire. He was introducing the new employee to a store owner. Frank wanted to be sure the new salesman got off on the right foot.

June was gathering up the dirty clothes to take to the basement to wash. Baxter followed her down the stairs. An ancient wringer washing machine had been left in the basement by the Shermans. Hilda had shown June how to use it.

June had just stepped off the last step onto the basement floor when she heard the guitar music again. She set down her basket of clothes and listened. She looked at the wall directly in front of her. Shelves to hold canning jars had been built on that side of the basement. In front of them were clothes lines. These were used to hang clothes in the winter when they could not be hung outdoors. She walked towards the front of the house. There was nothing there except some boxes resting on a work bench. They had been used to move things from the old house. She moved to the west side of the basement. The whole center of the basement was taken up by a huge coal furnace. A coal storage bin was on the west side.

She realized the music must be coming from the area of the cistern under the steps. On the back side of the basement was a no longer used cistern. Beside it sat the hot water heater. The inside walls of the cistern were one concrete block shorter than the basement walls.

June tried to look into the cistern but she was too short. She looked around the basement and found a pail. She tipped the pail over and put it next to the cistern wall, then stood on it. Standing on tippy-toes, she could just see into the cistern. Her eyes adjusted to the dark and she saw a window on the far side. It had a cracked pane. Part of the glass had fallen out. She saw a narrow ledge around the back wall. On this ledge sat an old guitar. She concluded, as wind moved in from the broken window it passed by the guitar vibrating the strings.

She climbed off the pail and stood quietly listening to the music. Baxter cocked his head and looked at June. She smiled at him saying, "Well, so much for a guitar-playing ghost. Just wait until I tell Frank! The sound is really quite pretty. If we try to get the guitar off the ledge it might break or fall. Besides, what will it hurt to leave it there? Frank doesn't seem so interested in it anyway. Maybe, I just won't say anything, unless he brings it up. Baxter, this will just be our secret."

The right conditions for the guitar playing seldom happened. The wind had to blow from the east. June also realized that the wind had to blow at a certain speed before the strings vibrated.

Chapter 10

Fall that year kept tugging summer along with it. June was walking to her in-laws to help Hilda can tomatoes. June had never canned anything and was looking forward to the experience. She arrived at a train crossing that had three tracks. Traffic was stopped as a train passed going west bound. Before it cleared the tracks an east bound train came rushing by. Traffic was building up on both sides of the tracks.

June heard her name being called above the noise of the trains. She looked over to the traffic and noticed someone waving to her. Walking over to the car she realized it was Donna Vandenburg, the church choir director. "Hi, Donna. How are you?"

"I'm just fine. Such a lovely day. I'm on my way to the church to sort through music. Where are you going? Can I give you a lift?"

June knew at the street on the other side of the tracks, Donna would be turning left to the church. June's in-laws lived down the street on the right. Not wanting to cause Donna unnecessary trouble she replied, "Thank you, so much. I'm just going to Hilda and Art's. It's no distance, I'll walk. We're canning tomatoes."

"Oh, this has been such a good year for tomatoes. I've already canned twenty-one quarts. If we don't have an early frost, I'm sure there will be more to put up."

The two trains cleared the tracks and the gates went up. Traffic was very backed up. The ladies said good-bye and Donna started across the tracks. The traffic in front of her stopped, waiting for a car to make a left turn at the intersection just beyond the tracks. The crossing signal went off and the gates started down. The gate on the opposite site of the road came down on top of the bed of a pick-up truck. June watched as the driver of the truck jumped out and ran just as a third train came barreling through.

Donna was trapped. There were cars in front of her and behind her. The train smashed into the truck and continued, crashing into Donna's car. It finally stopped several blocks down the tracks. A few road warriors, riding in boxcars jumped out. Most took off. One came up to June. She stood paralyzed.

"Lady are you alright? Can I do something

for you?" June looked up at his haggard, unshaven face. The man took her arm, giving it a shake, "Lady! Do you need help?"

No one noticed Mr. Duly come up. "Thank you, young man. I'll help the lady." "Here." Mr. Duly put the change from his pocket into the man's hand. The man tipped his hat and walked a few steps away, watching the gathering crowd.

Mr. duly put his arm around her, "June, let's go into my store and get out of this chaos."

She was led to an office and given a glass of water. "Shall I call Frank?"

"No, he's at a conference in Waterbury."

"How about I call Hilda and Art?" June only nodded.

The senior Grimes were a long time getting

to the store. The train still sat at the crossing. Streets were closed. Traffic was bedlam. They had to drive several miles around the city to get to the other side of the tracks. The traffic was still backed up. They finally parked their car in the J.C. Penney's® parking lot and walked the last three blocks to Duly's.

By the time they arrived there were police questioning June. Hilda heard Officer Jake Hutton asking June, "Are you sure you didn't hear a train whistle?"

"No! I've already told you. The two trains went by and cars started crossing the tracks. Then the gates came down again. The third train came and I thought, 'Where did that train come from.'"

"Okay, Mrs. Grimes, I want you to go home and relax. As soon as you feel able, please, write out a full description of what you saw. Give me a call when you have it done. Here is my card. I'll come by and get it."

The Sunday after the accident, the churches in town were full. A choir member at the Grimes's church led the singing in a very somber service. June sat listening to the solemn music. She never, ever told anyone, not even Frank, that Donna Vandenburg had offered her a ride.

Chapter 11

June's parents, Della and Charles Witherspoon and her brothers, Carl and Martin were coming for Thanksgiving. June was a bit apprehensive about their visit. This was a time of 'firsts' for her. It would be the first time she had seen her parents since the wedding. The two families would be meeting for the first time. This would also be the first time she had ever entertained anyone as a married woman. At the private school she had attended, she had learned all the proper basics of being a hostess. Knowing and doing were two different things.

June was still not a very good cook. She did have a brand new, "The Settlement Cook Book". It was subtitled "The Way to a Man's Heart". She relied heavily on this book. The directions for cooking a turkey were overwhelming. Hilda, once again, came to June's rescue. She volunteered to prepare the turkey for roasting. She planned to come over early on Thanksgiving Day to put it in the oven. Hilda was also bringing a sweet potato casserole and cranberries.

Mrs. Witherspoon was bringing the pies. June knew her mother's cook, Elena, would be the one making the pies. Mrs. Witherspoon never cooked and knew less about cooking than June. All June had to do was prepare a couple of vegetables and make rolls. She decided Swenson's Swedish Bakery would have better rolls than she could bake.

By late November, June had yet to be asked to substitute. She had about given up hope. Then, the Sunday evening before Thanksgiving the telephone rang. June thought it was probably Hilda or maybe her sister-in-law, Ruth. June hoped Ruth and Duke's plans had not changed. They were to celebrate Thanksgiving with his family. She liked them well enough, but really didn't want four more people to entertain.

Frank had been reading the paper and looked up as June picked up the telephone, "Hello, yes, this is Mrs. Grimes." June listened for several seconds, "Yes, I can. No, I can walk. Yes, yes. I'll be there. Good-bye. You have a good evening, also."

"What was that all about?"

"It was Miss Cantrell, the grade school principal. The third-grade teacher has taken ill and will be out all this week. Miss

Cantrell asked me to substitute for her. I told her I would." June sat on the edge of her chair holding her breath and waiting for Frank to say something.

"Well, that's nice. Maybe you can make enough money to get me a Christmas present. I know you will be able to teach one grade after handling eight. Let me know how I can help you get ready for Thanksgiving. You won't have much time to prepare."

"One thing you can do is ask Rev. Johnson if we can borrow a table and six chairs." He smirked at June and returned to his paper. With the paper still in front of his face, he said, "Okay I will."

June had no problem teaching the twenty-two third graders. She loved each one. Some she knew from her church. Tuesday afternoon, as she dismissed the class, she saw Miss Cantrell standing in the hall. June immediately hoped she had not done something wrong. All sorts of problems flashed through her mind. Had a parent complained about her? Were her lesson plans inadequate? Was there something wrong with her credentials?

Miss Cantrell bid each student good-by and said she hoped they had a nice Thanksgiving as they passed her on their way out. Finally, she looked at June, "Mrs. Grimes, let's go into your room. There is something I need to talk to you about."

June stepped aside and allowed Miss Cantrell to enter first. Miss Cantrell was a slim stately woman with dish water blond hair secured in a tightly wound bun. She had a high forehead and a very square jaw. June guessed her to be in her early thirties. Like June, she wore glasses.

Miss Cantrell turned, gave June her full attention and folded her hands in front of her. "I have been very pleased at how well you have done. You handle the students with wisdom and kindness."

"Thank you, Miss Cantrell." Internally, June sighed with relief. She then looked at Miss Cantrell and continued. "That is most kind of you. I truly enjoy teaching."

"I'm glad to hear that. Anyone can see how much you enjoy being here. Now I must tell you the reason for my requesting this conversation. Miss Jackson, the regular teacher telephoned me. She is quite ill. She has not improved and will be undergoing surgery. She is not sure when or even if she will be able to return to her position this year."

June lifted her right hand to the side of her

face and with sincere emotion replied, "Oh, how awful."

"Yes, it is. She has had a number of episodes, leading up to her present condition, during this school year. If this recent bout had not occurred, I was going to have to talk to her about her numerous absences. It was only with this last siege she finally confided in me about the cause." Neither did Miss Cantrell elaborate on the cause of Miss Jackson's illness, nor did June feel it appropriate to question her.

"Having said that, brings us to you. I know you only signed up to substitute a couple of days each week. But the school, the students, and I need your help. Would you consider teaching full-time, until Miss Jackson is able to return? You must realize she may not return to school this year."

June wanted to shout 'hallelujah'. At

the same time, she felt a guilty joy at the expense of Miss Jackson's pain. She managed to stay composed, "Miss Cantrell, I am truly very sorry you are offering me this position because of Miss Jackson's illness. I wouldn't wish this problem on her just so I can teach. I do so much enjoy teaching and want to accept the position. First, I must discuss this with my husband to be sure he is in agreement with me. Knowing the kind of man he is, I believe he will not have a problem with my teaching full-time".

June was right. Frank was all for her bringing in extra money. She accepted the position. The only thing that upset her was the fact she would continue to be paid as a substitute teacher which was $10.00 a day. The regular full-time teachers with three years' experience, which June had, were paid at the rate of about $13.00 a day.

The Wednesday before Thanksgiving dawned gray and cold. It had snowed most of the night. The wind began to howl with the coming of daylight. June watched from the living room front window as a snow plow cleared the street. Almost as soon as the plow disappeared in the blowing snow, the street was again covered with more snow. Frank had taken the day off so he could help get things ready for tomorrow. He came into the room carrying two cups of coffee. He sat down in front of the fireplace. Green wood popped as water trapped within the wood turned to steam and expanded. "Come over here and have some coffee before you get ready for school. Listen to that wood. Next time I get a load, I'll be sure it's better seasoned."

"I'm worried my folks aren't going to get here. The roads must be terrible."

"Well, there's not much we can do about it." As Frank was talking, the telephone rang." June grabbed it before Frank had a chance.

"Hello. Oh, good morning if that's what you can call it."

Hilda was on the other end. "This is the day which the Lord hath made; we will rejoice and be glad in it."

"Thanks Hilda. I needed that. Where is that verse? I think I'll make it one of my favorites.

"It's Psalm 118:24. I think you should call your folks and tell them not to come. We can celebrate Thanksgiving on Friday or even Saturday or Sunday."

"That's probably a good idea. Will the turkey keep?"

"Yes, it'll keep in the fridge for a while."

Thanksgiving was finally celebrated on Saturday. Art Grimes and Charles Witherspoon hit it off instantly. They both enjoyed playing checkers. They played several games. Art won most of them.

Hilda and Della Witherspoon were a bit more reserved with each other. They really had very little in common. Della did not feel comfortable in the kitchen. Fortunately, Ruth and her family had come. Mrs. Witherspoon enjoyed children and took over entertaining Everett. They spent a good part of the day playing Chutes & Ladders and building with Lincoln Logs.

Duke appropriated June's brothers, taking them bowling after the meal. They didn't get back until late Saturday night. June heard them come in. Then she heard her father talking softly to the boys.

Everyone went to church Sunday morning including Frank and Duke and two very tired young men. June was so pleased at how the week-end had gone. Even having Ruth and her family come had resulted in a blessing. She wondered what her father had said to her brothers. Monday morning, she wasn't sure who was more tired, her students or her.

 **Chapter 12**

One evening, just after New Year's Day, June sat at the kitchen table writing lesson plans. Frank had to stay at work to help with inventory. Baxter lay sleeping on a rug in front of the sink. Suddenly he jumped up and looked startled. "What is it Baxter?" No sooner had she said this, when she heard footsteps at the back door. "Is Frank home already? I guess he didn't have to work as late as he thought."

June went to the door and opened it. A rough hand grabbed her, pushing her back into the kitchen. It was Eddie Stover, the son of Ella, who owned the Painted Porch.

"Eddie, what are you doing here? Let me go! You're hurting my arm!"

Baxter leaped off the rug biting into Eddie's leg. Eddie let out a terrific wail. He let go of June's arm and fell to the floor. Baxter continued to growl, and hold on to the leg, shaking his head from side to side. June was not sure what to do. She saw the meat mallet drying in the dish drainer. She grabbed it thinking she could use it as a weapon if necessary. She then grabbed Baxter's collar. "No, Baxter! Stop! Drop it! Let go!" June pulled Baxter away from Eddie. She hung on to Baxter's collar and managed to drag him into the dining room.

Not letting go of Baxter's collar, she slammed the door between the two rooms and locked it. Next, dragging Baxter with her as he continued trying to return to the kitchen, she went to the telephone in the living room. She dialed the operator, "This is Mrs. Grimes at 503 Fir Ave. I have an emergency. I need the police and an ambulance."

June could hear Eddie crying, "I just wanted to be your friend. Help me! Help me! I want my mama". June wanted to go to the kitchen to see how badly Eddie was hurt but was afraid she would not be able to control Baxter.

It was only minutes before two policemen arrived, followed shortly by an ambulance. It was the same two officers, Jake Hutton and Michael Smith, who had answered the call the time she had been chased when living at the old house. The flashing light had attracted several neighbors who were soon congregated about the yard.

"Eddie Stover is in the kitchen. He's hurt. I think he might be the same man who attacked Baxter and chased me last summer. Let me put the dog in the bedroom. I'm afraid he will attack Eddie again."

Once Baxter was secured, June unlocked the kitchen door. Eddie was lying in a pool of his blood, holding his leg, and crying. "Mrs. Grimes, I just wanted to be your friend. I like you. I thought you would be my friend. Why did your dog bite me?"

The ambulance attendant gave Eddie first-aid. June knelt down beside Eddie. "You don't make a friend by grabbing and hurting them. Eddie, are you the person who hit the dog and chased me last summer?"

Eddie started crying uncontrollably, "That man's hurting me. Make him stop. I want to go home. I want my mama."

"Eddie, the man is helping you. He has to stop the bleeding."

Jake Hutton, the older of the two policemen was very compassionate, "Mrs. Grimes, come back into the living room. Eddie isn't able to rationally make sense of anything. Let the attendant get him fixed up. We'll get him to the hospital and call his mama."

The younger policeman, Michael Smith, led June back into the living room. She sat down and began to shake. What had happened to her again, suddenly registered. "Are you okay Mrs. Grimes? Do you need medical attention?" The whole time Baxter was heard banging against the bedroom door and barking.

"Just a glass of water, please. The bathroom is straight through there." June pointed to the small alcove. The policeman left to get her a drink. He returned and handed her a glass just as the front door opened and Frank rushed in. "Frank, oh Frank! It's Eddie! I think he's the one who hit Baxter and chased me last summer. Baxter needs to be let out before he breaks down the door."

Frank ignored Baxter and knelt beside June's chair. He turned as two attendants wearing parkas over white uniforms wheeled out a stretcher holding Eddie. "Oh, poor Eddie," moaned June. She leaned her head back and closed her eyes. She really felt terrible.

Jake Hutton entered the living room and noticed June's distress, "Mrs. Grimes, do you need to go to the hospital for a check-up?"

"No, Officer Hutton, thank you. I'll be fine. I

just need to get my bearings. What's going to happen to Eddie?"

"Well, do you want to press charges?"

Frank stood up, "Of course we do. He's dangerous and needs to be put away."

Although June did not feel up to a confrontation, she knew she had to speak up. "I'm not sure that is the best thing to do."

"What are you talking about? The man breaks into our house and attacks you. And you don't want to have him arrested?"

"He didn't break in. I heard him at the back door and thought it was you. I opened the door and, yes, he did grab my arm. But I don't believe he really meant it as an attack. In his mind, he's like a child. He doesn't know or understand the proper way to behave."

"He can't just be left to go around grabbing people," protested Frank.

"I agree. I'd like to talk to his mother. Maybe there is some kind of help he can get." June turned to Officer Hutton, "What can you tell us about him? Has this been a problem in the past?"

"When he was a teen-ager, there were a couple of incidents with some girls. Nothing serious. It was mostly caused from the other teens, boys and girls, teasing him to the point that he struck out at them. Since then, his family has kept a pretty close watch on him. He normally stays home. He must have started sneaking out at night."

"Frank, let's wait. Let me talk to his mother."

Frank gave an exasperated groan, "I

suppose. But I don't like the idea. I say lock him up and throw away the key."

 **Chapter 13**

June spent a restless night. She really was miserable. At dawn, she dragged herself out of bed. Frank was already up. She could hear him in the kitchen making coffee. The thought of coffee made her nauseous. She swallowed a couple of times and took a shower.

June called The Painted Porch before leaving for school. Stella answered. She said Eddie would have to be in the hospital for several days. June asked to visit Eddie's mother, Ella, after school. Stella said her sister was still at the hospital but expected her home soon. Stella said she would be sure Ella was home to see June.

Since Frank drove their only car to his work, June called Hilda. She asked Hilda to drive her out to see Ella after school. June told her mother-in-law, there was strength in numbers.

Hilda had heard about Eddie's attack on the radio's morning news and was willing to drive June.

Hilda was waiting at the school when June walked out. They talked about the problem on the drive to the farm. "June, do you think Eddie is mentally ill and should be committed to a state mental hospital?"

"No, I don't. He's mentally deficient. That's different. He wouldn't get the help he needs at a mental hospital. They might give him shock treatments or some other therapy. I doubt it would help him."

Hilda looked at June, "You're educated, do you think there's anything that can be done for someone like him?"

"It depends on what Mrs. Stover wants. I talked to Miss Cantrell, the school principal. She wasn't very encouraging. She remembered Eddie. It was her first-year teaching. Eddie was enrolled in kindergarten. After only a few days the teacher sent his mother a note, pinned to Eddie's shirt. It said there wasn't anything she could do for Eddie and not to send him back to school again."

"I seem to remember something about that. Honestly, I'm not surprised."

"Yes, when a teacher has a room of twenty or more children, she really doesn't have the time or expertise to focus on someone like Eddie. Miss Cantrell said Eddie's intelligence is only about that of a three-year-old." June sighed as she said this.

"I can't believe there isn't something available to help a person like Eddie. Do you know of anything June?"

"There are some institutions for people like Eddie. However, many of them are actually cruel and degrading places. There are all kinds of dreadful things that happen to the patients. They have even been used for medical experiments. If a patient is violent, he might be given a lobotomy which is cutting out the front part of the brain. Sometimes they are used for forced labor, or not well fed and even sometimes tied to their beds."

"Oh my. That's terrible!"

"When I talked to Miss Cantrell, she did say there are some church-sponsored institutions with good reputations. She even volunteered to do some inquiries for me. I think she likes me."

The two women drove down the snow-covered road, now lined with trees devoid of their leaves. Before the ladies were out of the car, Ella Stover was out the front door and heading toward them. She reached June before she had the car door closed. Ella took hold of June's hands and started crying, "Mrs. Grimes, I'm so, so sorry. I've tried so hard to keep Eddie here. I even lock his bedroom door at night. He must have climbed out the window." She dropped to her knees in the mud and snow, still holding June's hands, she pleaded, "Please, don't have him arrested. Please."

June took Ella by the elbows, helping her to

stand. "Mrs. Stover, I'm not going to press charges. I know it wouldn't help anything." Having said that, Ella started crying harder.

By this time Hilda had come around to the passenger side of the car, "Ella, let's go into the house where it's warm and we can sit down."

Once inside and seated around a lovely old Queen Anne piecrust table, Stella came in with hot tea and shortbread cookies. June was very thankful as she had not eaten very much that day. Stella talked while serving, "Something has to be done. We hardly had any guests today. Ladies are getting afraid to come out here."

Ella continued to weep, "I don't know what to do. I just don't."

"Mrs. Stover, I took it upon myself to seek some advice from Miss Cantrell, the grade school principal. She is investigating church-sponsored residential homes for people like Eddie."

"Oh, I've heard horrible things about places like that. I couldn't send him to one of those. Besides, how would I ever afford to pay for such a place?"

"Some do have bad reputations. But the church affiliated ones have some good results."

"The good ones are going to be too expensive and too far away. I'll never get to see my Eddie again." Ella started crying hard again.

Stella grabbed Ella by the shoulders, "Ella! Stop bawling. Are you going to wait until Eddie does something really bad or hurts someone or even himself seriously? He can't stay here. You've already seen how people are afraid to come to the restaurant. Our business will close. I'm going to call Uncle Clarence." Stella turned to June. "Uncle Clarence is our father's brother. He's never married and has more money than he knows what to do with. I know he can afford to help, if he's willing."

Ella stopped crying and looked at her sister, then at June. "How long do you think it will be before the principal has information for us?"

"I really don't know."

Two weeks later Miss Cantrell came to June's classroom and beckoned her into the hall. "I've found a church sponsored residential home for children like Eddie. They call all their residents children, no matter how old they are. I understand some of them are as old as sixty or more." She handed June a beautiful brochure. Pictured was a lovely two-story brick building, play grounds and tree-shaded walks.

"This looks lovely if the pictures are true. This says the boys are taught farming and gardening. Eddie would like that. He loves his flowers. And, it's only seventy-five miles away! Mrs. Stover will be glad to know that. But, oh, look at the price. I doubt if Mrs. Stover can afford this."

"June, it really isn't your problem. Take the brochure to her and let her decide."

Stella convinced her Uncle Clarence to pay for Eddie's care. He arrived in his black 1939 V12 Packard Club Sedan to drive Eddie and Ella to the facility. Ella was nervous and fidgety. She was frightened for Eddie. Eddie thought it was grand; he was going to go for a ride in his great-uncle's fancy car. Ella could not stop thanking her uncle for his generosity. Finally, Uncle Clarence had enough of her excess appreciativeness, "Enough caterwauling, Ella. It's past time the boy was committed."

Ella was about to express her resentment at her uncle's choice of words when Stella grabbed her arm, squeezing it painfully. Ella looked at her sister and saw a look of admonishment.

 **Chapter 14**

By the first of February, June was sure she was pregnant. The week following, at her doctor's appointment, it was confirmed. Her due date was September 5, 1939. Frank was over the moon, "If it's a boy, let's name him Russell. I've always liked the name Rusty."

June laughed. She was so happy for Frank. She hoped she did have a boy, just for Frank. What she was troubled about was telling Miss Cantrell. June could just hear Miss Cantrell, "Well, that's why we don't like to employ married women!"

June went to see Miss Cantrell. She quietly stood in the open doorway. The principal was sitting behind her desk, writing. She looked up and saw June. "Come in, June and sit down. What can I do for you?" June sat down putting her hands in her lap. She looked at Miss Cantrell. She could not seem to find her voice. Miss Cantrell looked directly at June, "Is there something you need to tell me?"

"What a pro she is! She already knows," thought June. "Yes, Miss Cantrell. I'm going to have a baby." She paused before continuing. "The baby isn't due until September. I can finish out the semester."

"Well, yes, Mrs. Grimes, I guess congratulations are in order. I can't say I'm surprised. It's a natural thing to happen. As to finishing out the year; I'll have to take it up with Mr. Neuman, the superintendent. He'll have to talk to the school board."

"I've been feeling fine. I haven't been sick or anything. I'm keeping up with my school work."

"It's not particularly that. It's more to do with your physical appearance. The problem will be when you start…ah…, when you have to wear maternity clothes." June sat and stared at Miss Cantrell. June was speechless.

"I want you to know I think you are an excellent teacher. I would really like to keep you here. I will tell Mr. Neuman how pleased I am with you."

"Thank you, Miss Cantrell. I appreciate your kind words."

June went home that evening depressed. After supper she sat in her chair by the fireplace reading the newspaper. She came to an advertisement for women's suits. Several of the jackets had pleats in the back making them rather boxy looking. She had an idea. The next Saturday she went to The Farris Fabric Store and bought a suit pattern and material for four garments. As she finished each suit, she started wearing it to school. She made each one out of such material that she could interchange jackets with different skirts. This gave her a number of various outfits. She wore these garments the rest of the school year. No one could tell if she was "showing" or not. Miss Cantrell never brought up the subject, either.

September 1st, 1939, Germany invaded Poland and England declared war on Germany. It was the beginning of the Second World War. That same day Russell

Arthur Grimes invaded the Grimes family, weighing six pounds, fourteen ounces.

June realized she knew very little about caring for an infant. Her brothers had a nurse until they were two-years-old. Their nurses had done everything for them. June was only permitted to hold the babies if she were sitting.

In 1939, most new mothers stayed in the hospital for ten days. During this confinement classes on infant care were taught. June attended all of them. Some of them she went to more than once. The classes consisted of infant feeding and possible problems that may be encountered such as reflex vomiting, diarrhea, and colic. She learned how to bathe and dress an infant, even how to wrap a baby in a blanket so he would feel secure. A nurse covered diaper rash, cradle cap (a condition June had never heard of), excessive crying, teething, infant milestones, and childhood infections. Since she had a boy, she and Frank had to decide if he would be circumcised.

Rusty was healthy and energetic. He never seemed to quit moving. June had thought he kicked a lot before he was born. Now he seemed never to stop kicking and constantly moving his arms and legs. June worried something might be wrong with him. When she questioned the doctor, he smiled and answered, "No, some babies just like to move. Maybe he's going to be a runner."

Della, June's mother encouraged her to hire a nurse. She even offered to pay for one. But June enjoyed being a mother. Each day was a new adventure. She marveled as Rusty developed new skills.

Frank said he believed Rusty must be the smartest baby ever born. Art and Hilda came over almost daily. Hilda was a blessing to June. She thanked God every day for giving her such a wonderful mother-in-law.

Each evening after putting Russell to bed for the night, Frank and June listened to all the news coming from Europe on the radio. War developments marred an otherwise happy family.

Vivian June Grimes lustily made her entrance on December 7, 1941, the same day Japan attacked Pearl Harbor, Hawaii. The next day, the United States entered the war. When Frank was finally allowed to visit June, he smiled a proud-papa smile at June, then told her, "Honey, I don't think we had better have any more children. Every time we do, a war starts."

He made light of the situation but June had darker thoughts. "Do you think you'll get drafted?"

"Me! June, I'm thirty-four, married and the father of two kids. The army doesn't want an old man like me. And even if I did get drafted, I'd be sitting at a desk shuffling papers, not carrying a gun." He was wrong on both counts.

 **Chapter 15**

Frank was working long hours in his position as manager. Several of the workers had volunteered for military service. Others were being drafted. The company had even hired women workers including some whose husbands had been drafted. All too frequently one of the women would call off. She had received a dreaded telegram informing her of her husband or son's death. On these occasions, Frank found it necessary to work on the packaging lines. He always gave credit for the work done to the grieving employee.

At a company meeting in the early spring of 1943, the company's president presented the need for more storage space. Frank hesitated for only a minute. "Mr. MacMillan?"

"Yes, Frank. Do you have a suggestion?"

"I am reluctant to say this. I don't want anyone to think I'm trying to make profit off the war."

"Yes, yes, what is it?"

"I still own a house and five acres on the west end of town. No one lives in the house. It's sort of run down. And it isn't very large. But it is just across the street from the train tracks. It might do until a better place is found."

"Mr. MacMillan, I know that place." Mr. Reimann, the vice-president, spoke up. "It might serve us well. And we could put up some temporary buildings on the vacant five acres. We can see if we can get a train spur built. That would be really convenient."

Mr. MacMillan tapped his pencil on the table. A habit which irritated his secretary as this caused the lead in the pencil to break. Her boss continually complained, telling her to buy better pencils. Finally, he stood up, "Let's go look at it."

Several voices said in unison, "Right now?"

"No time like the present."

Frank's company leased the house and land for a very good price. Frank was reluctant at first to accept the offer. Mr. MacMillan told him; he was being foolish and financially unwise. No one knew what tomorrow would bring.

June was no longer teaching school. She

was glad to be able to be a stay-at-home mom. She was faced with another vacant land situation. Behind the Grimes's home on Fir Avenue was a vacant lot. At the far end the city had dug a ditch in an effort to prevent flooding in the area. The sides of the ditch had been built up and were higher than the surrounding land. Water was actually pumped up into the ditch.

Four-year-old Rusty loved to play outdoors. He was a bold and daring little boy. It was an effort for June to keep track of him. So, he would not go over to the drainage ditch, she told him the empty lot separating the house from the ditch had snakes in it. And if Rusty were to venture into the lot, he might get bitten.

Years later Rusty confronted his mother about her false tale. She defended herself by telling him, she did it to protect him from drowning. He retorted, "Yeah, but because of that, I've always been afraid of snakes."

June replied, "What I did, I did for love. One night, when you were about two, a couple of teen-age boys drove a car up and down the sides of the ditch. The driver lost control and the car flipped over into the ditch. It was two days before the car was discovered. The boys had drowned. Maybe letting you believe there were snakes in the vacant lot saved you from drowning."

It was July 23, 1943, and June was watching for the mailman. Her brother, Carl, was serving in the Navy. She had not received a letter from him in almost a month. She saw the mailman leaving her neighbor, Mable Cunningham's house, and opened her front door to wait for him.

"Good morning Mrs. Grimes. Expecting a letter, are yah?"

"Yes, Jim, from my brother."

"I think there might be one here."

June took the mail and looked at Jim. He had an odd look on his face. He tipped his hat and hurried down the steps.

June went into the house and shuffled through the mail until she came to one addressed to Frank. She stared at the return address, Selective Service, Local Board, Fairview. She started to shake and slumped into a chair. June's daughter nick-named Vivi, was under the dining room table playing house. Rusty was playing with a new puppy by the fireplace. Baxter had died just before Christmas of 1942. Rusty noted the odd look on June's face, "What's the matter Mommie? You look all white."

"Nothing Rusty. Mommie's fine." She placed the letter on the mantel. A still small voice echoed in her mind, "Nothing is going to happen that God can't handle, and God won't give me more than I can handle."

June prepared Frank's favorite meal for supper, spaghetti and meatballs. Frank smelled it as soon as he opened the door. "Oh boy, Honey. That smells great! What's the occasion? You're not pregnant again, are you?"

June smiled, wishing she were, "No, Darling. There's a letter for you on the mantel." As soon as she spoke, she wished she had waited until after supper.

Frank took one look at it and gave June a sickly smile. "Well, I guess I was wrong about the army not wanting old men." He opened the envelope. The first thing he noticed typed across the top in all capital letters was: 'YOU MUST ACKNOWLEDGE THIS BY TELEPHONE, THIS OFFICE (2-8155) ON OR BEFORE AUGUST 1, 1943.' It was dated July 21, 1943. Again, in bold letters it continued: 'ORDER TO REPORT FOR INDUCTION.' The body of the letter read;

The President of the United States,

To Frank Grimes

GREETING:

Frank didn't have to read any more, he knew what it said. Less than two weeks later he was on a bus headed for basic training.

At the training camp, most of the other recruits were nineteen and twenty years old. Only one other man was near Frank's age, Merle Gibson. Merle was twenty-six, which the younger men thought was old. Merle was from Montana, a real cowboy. He had grown up on a working ranch, bulldogging cattle, mending fences, digging wells, preparing his own meals, sleeping outdoors, building barns, and doing all the other chores related to ranching. He was not physically challenged as was Frank. Frank could not believe how "out of shape" he had become. The younger men called him Gramps.

Frank and Merle became good friends. Frank wrote home to June, "If it wasn't for Merle's help and encouragement, I doubt I would have made it through basic."

After basic training, both were assigned to the Quartermaster Corps. Except for ammunition and medical stores, the Quartermaster Corps supplied all general supplies needed to keep the army going such as meals, petroleum, water, clothing and shoes. They also buried the dead in temporary graves.

Thanksgiving, 1943, was a difficult one. Fortunately, Frank was stationed only a long bus ride from home. He was given a three-day pass before being shipped out to the Pacific. Everyone tried to make it a good Thanksgiving.

Frank's mother and dad hosted a Thanksgiving family dinner. The government was rationing most food products. Rationing meant a person had to have enough ration stamps to put with the cash of a rationed item before being allowed to purchase it. Sugar, eggs, milk, tea, coffee, and meat were among food items rationed.

Earlier that summer, Hilda, June and Ruth had planted a "victory garden". They had a bumper crop of vegetables and strawberries. By combining their ration stamps, the three women were able to buy enough ingredients to make several pies from the strawberries they had grown and canned. Somehow Hilda had managed to purchase a beautiful turkey. All the adults pretended to be having a good time, for the children's sake.

June thought back to the first Thanksgiving dinner she had hosted as a new bride. This Thanksgiving was so very different. She tried to pretend to be happy. Inside she was crying and scared. What was going to happen? She did not want Frank to go to war. The few months since he had left for training had been so lonely and difficult. Rusty and Vivi didn't understand. Rusty kept asking for his daddy. There were so many chores that Frank had done. Now she was having to do them. With the loss of income from

Frank's job, she decided to return to substitute teach. "Oh, God," she prayed. "Please help me."

 **Chapter 16**

Frank was good about writing letters to June and his folks. His letters were always positive. He assured them he was several miles behind any fighting. He could not tell them where he was or his exact job. He only said the weather was fine and he was working to keep the "fighting men" supplied with food and fuel.

June prayed for Frank several times each day. She prayed for families with a blue or gold star in a window even if she did not know the family. A blue star hung in her window. More and more gold stars were replacing blue ones. This meant a service man in a family had died. If she was out walking and a telegraph boy passed her on his bicycle, she prayed for the boy delivering the telegram and the family receiving it. She knew it most likely meant a loved one was dead, wounded or missing.

May 20, 1944, dawned gray and cold. It had rained most of the night. June was getting Rusty and Vivi ready for the day when the doorbell rang. Who could be calling so early in the morning? She had a sinking feeling in the pit of her stomach. A boy from Western Union® stood at the door when June opened it. He shoved a telegram in her hand and quickly left.

June watched him leave. "No, God please, no." She stood silently watching the boy ride away. Rusty tugged at her dress.

"Mommie, what's the matter? Who was at the door? What's in your hand?"

It seemed all Rusty did lately was ask questions. He would be starting kindergarten this fall. "Nothing's wrong Sweetie. Please go and help Vivi put on her shoes." Rusty's older cousin, Everett, had taught Rusty to tie shoes recently. He loved to help June tie her apron, and Vivi's shoes or anything else he could find that needed tying.

June walked to her chair, sank down and stared at the envelope. Once again, she prayed before opening it. "Dear God, whatever is in this telegram, help me, please." Slowly she pulled up the flap and looked at the words. Frank was missing in action. How could it be? In all his letters, he had assured her he was in a safe place, just filling procurement requisitions.

A car drove into the driveway. June knew before she went to the door who it was. She took a deep, calming breath and walked to the door. Thinking she had herself under control, as soon as she opened the door she burst into tears. Hilda took June in her arms and held her tightly. They stood silently embracing each other; each trying to put on a brave face.

"June, he isn't dead. He's someplace. They'll find him and he'll come home. I know he will."

Rusty and Vivi came running from the bedroom. Grandpa Grimes caught up Vivi as she ran into his arms. "Hey kids, let's go get some doughnuts for breakfast." Art put the children's coats on them, then took his two grandchildren out to his car and headed for Swenson's Swedish Bakery.

June collapsed in her favorite chair and

looked at her mother-in-law with tears in her eyes. After some time, June spoke, "What are we going to do? What will I tell the children?"

"We must go on just as we have been. Keep writing letters to Frank. Do what you have been doing with the children. Right now, they don't need to know. Besides they're too young to understand, anyway."

That was exactly what June did. She continued to write to Frank telling him about the children and what they were doing. She got more involved in the church and the activities to aid the GIs, such as: knitting socks, collecting newspapers, and saving lard drippings.

The church announced a scrap drive. June didn't have much to give as scrap. She had the children get Rusty's red wagon. They walked around the community collecting tin cans, used auto parts, broken tools and something unrecognizable. The giver assured June it was made of medal.

She also fasted several meals each week. Instead of eating, she spent time in prayer for Frank and other needs as God made them known to her. As the war raged on her prayer list became longer and longer.

For several weeks a problem had been brewing. Gaylen Browne, an old bachelor, lived on the other side of the Cunninghams. He had been purposely walking up and down the sidewalk. He walked past the Grimes's house and back to his house. If he saw June, he would stop, smile and wave to her. One evening in February of 1945, June had just finished the supper dishes. Five-year-old, Rusty was listening to "The Lone Ranger" on the radio. Vivi age two was playing with her dolls. As June walked into the living room the doorbell rang. She had come to dread that bell.

Standing on the porch and holding a mixed bouquet of flowers was Gaylen Browne. June didn't know him well. She knew he was retired from some factory job on the southside of town. He was very tall, with a long face and piercing dark eyes, "Good evening, Mr. Browne. What a surprise. What can I do for you?"

"May I come in? I bought these flowers for you."

Alarm bells sounded in June's head. "They are lovely. However, I don't feel it would be appropriate for you to come in or for me to accept such a gift. Why don't you donate them to your church?"

"Now Mrs. Grimes, June, I've been

watching you for some time. I know you are probably a widow. I just want us to get to know each other better. To become friends. And please call me Gaylen."

"Mr. Browne, please leave. I am not interested in your attention." Having said that, June closed the door leaving him standing on the porch. She walked to her favorite chair and sat staring at her wedding rings. She reminisced about the day Frank had taken her to Ackermann's Fine Jewelry Store in Ravensburg.

June remembered Frank telling her, he had gone to Ackermann's and had already picked out several rings. He assured June that if she didn't like any of them, she could ask to see others. She understood that meant Frank had already talked to Mr. Ackermann about how much he could spend. She would only be shown rings in that price category. June really didn't mind.

After viewing the diamonds, which were small, June stated what she would really like was a pearl. Her birthstone was pearl and she had wanted a pearl ring for several years.

Mr. Ackermann smiled at June, "I think I have a ring you might really like. Just a minute please." He left and returned with a yellow gold ring. A large pearl occupied the center with two small sapphires on either side. "This ring is 18K gold. Made by the French jewelry company Mauboussin in about 1860. It is a natural south sea pearl. All three stones are of exceptional quality."

"Oh, it's beautiful. Do you know anything about its provenance?"

"Yes, I do. What I am going to tell you is

in confidence. I believe I can trust you not to tell others." He gave June and Frank a stern look. Both nodded. "You know Mrs. Wellington?"

"Of course. She is the rich lady that donated the land to build the school where I teach. The board had planned to erect just one room. She gave money so the building could be made larger and used as a community center."

"That's right. However, she was not as rich as most people thought. She came to me to sell most of her jewelry to finance the enlargement. This ring is the best piece she had."

June turned to Frank, "This is the ring I want. Besides being beautiful, it has such a wonderful story. I feel connected to it."

Frank picked up the ring giving it a good

look, "Mr. Ackermann what kind of blue stones did you say these are?"

"They're sapphires."

"Isn't that September's birthstone?"

"Yes, why."

June spoke before Frank had a chance, "That's your birth month!"

June selected a plain gold band for her wedding band. When her mother had seen the engagement ring for the first time, she had been disappointed and seemed almost ashamed of it. A couple of years ago, Frank had offered to get her a new diamond ring. She said no, she loved her ring.

Getting out of her chair, June sighed, made sure all the doors were locked and turned out the lights before going to bed. How she dreaded sleeping in that double bed alone, again.

The next morning Mabel Cunningham knocked at her back door. June was in the kitchen ironing. She sat the iron on its heel and went to the door, hoping it wasn't Gaylen Browne. "Good morning, Mabel. It's nice to see you. Please, come in. I was about to take a break. Join me in a cup of coffee, such as it is." Coffee was one of the rationed products, scarce and expensive. June was buying Postum®, a coffee substitute made of wheat bran and molasses.

"Yes, I'd like a cup. I can't stay long. Barney and I are going out to my sisters. She raises chickens. Would you like me to bring you back a few eggs?"

"That would be much appreciated. How much do they cost?"

"I'll let you know when I get back. She may just give me some, if the hens are laying well. What I really came to see you about is Gaylen Browne. I saw him at your door last night."

June had turned off the iron and was pouring coffee as Mabel talked. Both ladies sat down at the kitchen table. Neither one put sugar or cream in their coffee. Both knew sugar and cream were hard to come by.

"June, I came to warn you. Stay away from Browne. He's no good."

June looked at Mabel disconcerted, "I have no intention of being friends with him or any man. I did not ask or expect him to be at my door last night."

"I'm sorry. That didn't come out the way I meant. I know you are a wholesome, upright Christian that wouldn't do anything wrong. I just felt it necessary to caution you about him. He isn't nice. Barney and I have suffered through ten years of him being our neighbor. Barney has been in his house once to help with some problem. He said that he has awful pictures of naked women hanging. He refused to ever go in that house again."

"Thank you for caring. I will be very careful to watch out for him."

They talked on about 'what is the world coming to,' the war, children, and other topics of concern to women at that time. A horn sounded in the Cunningham driveway. "That's Barney. I must go. Please be careful."

June didn't give Gaylen Browne much thought during the following days. About a week later, she and Rusty were walking to Ruth's to pick up Vivi. June walked to school and any other place she could. Gas was rationed and tires were difficult to replace. A light drizzle was falling. June had been substituting at Rusty's school that day. Vivi stayed with her Aunt Ruth. June heard a car horn tooting. It pulled up beside June and Rusty as the window was rolled down. "Hop in. I'll give you a lift." It was Browne. Rusty made a move to the car. June grabbed his coat collar and pulled him back.

"No thanks, that's not necessary. We're on our way to get my daughter, then I have some shopping to do."

"I'm not in any hurry. Let me take you around. You're getting all wet."

"Mr. Browne, the longer we stand here the wetter we get. Now good day." June

grabbed Rusty's arm and propelled
him along.

Rusty looked questioningly at his mom,
"What's wrong with getting a ride from Mr.
Browne? He's real nice. He gives us candy."

June stopped and looked at her son.
"What! He gives you candy?"

"Sure, sometimes when we're out playing,
he'll call us over to his house. We go in and
he passes out candy to us."

"Listen Rusty. I don't ever want you to go
into his house again. Nor are you to take
candy from him or any man without my
permission. Do you understand me?"

"Sure Mom. But why?"

"Because I said so. That's why."

June continued to substitute almost every
day. After getting home from school she

still had meals to prepare and house work to do. Sometimes she felt overwhelmed. Mr. Browne was put out of her mind. That was until early one evening when the telephone rang.

"Hello."

"Good evening, Mrs. Grimes. This is Gaylen Browne. It's such a nice evening I was hoping you and the children would have supper with me and maybe take in a movie."

"Mr. Browne, stop calling me. This is the third time this week you've called. I've seen you on the sidewalk watching my house. Stop coming to my house. And stop giving my children candy. I am not interested in you. If you continue to bother me, I will report you to the police. Good night." She thumped down the receiver.

Continuing to sit and stare at the telephone she was unsure what to do. He probably hadn't broken any laws. So, it wouldn't do to call the police. She got up, checked all the doors and windows to assure they were locked. "Oh Frank, how I miss you. God, please watch over the children and me."

She returned to her chair putting her hand up to her forehead and began to cry. She had not noticed the children watching wide eyed from their bedroom door.

They rushed over to their mother. Rusty put his hand on June's arm, "Please don't cry Mommie. I'll protect you."

Vivi was standing holding her doll and crying. June gathered her children on her lap and held them tightly. Just then the doorbell rang. She put the children down. "Go to your room."

The two stood staring at her as the bell went off again. "Now!" They hurried to their room.

June marched to the door shouting, "Mr. Browne I told you to leave us alone. I'm calling the police. Go away!"

Hilda began to loudly call, "June it's Hilda and Art. Open the door. What's wrong?"

June unlocked the door and fell into Hilda's arms. The children came running out of their room. "Oh Grandpa, I'm so glad you're here. Mr. Browne is bothering Mommie and is trying to get in the house." This was volunteered by Rusty.

"What!" exclaimed Hilda. June took her handkerchief and wiped her eyes then straightened her hair with her hand. She then explained what was going on as the group continued to stand in the middle of the living room, except Vivi. She had reached out her arms to her grandpa and had been picked up.

Art put Vivi down then said, "Tell you what. Let's have a pajama party. You kids get your pj's and tooth brushes. We'll go to our house, pop some corn, and play checkers."

Rusty had started towards his bedroom. He turned and looked at his grandpa, "Could we play dominos instead. You always win at checkers."

"Sure. Now go get your jams. June get what you need and lock up. I'll take care of Gaylen Browne.

The next day was Saturday. June and the children stayed at the senior Grimes. To the surprise of Hilda, Art; his son-in-law, Duke Pember, and Barney Cunningham visited Gaylen Browne. Art was always so quiet, and mild-mannered. Hilda was proud of her husband that day for standing up to Browne. Before the day was done Gaylen Browne had left town. June never learned what was said to him.

One day when June was substituting, another teacher, Elsa Warren approached her. "Don't you live on Fir Avenue?" Before June could answer, Elsa continued, "Did you know a man by the name of Gordon, or maybe it is Godfrey Browne?"

"His name is Gaylen Browne. He lived two houses down from me. Why?"

"Well, my sister's brother-in-law is Clyde Everard, the real estate owner. He told my sister that this Browne fellow asked his agency to sell his house. But before it could be put on the market, Clyde had to hire a company to come in and clean it. My sister said it was so grimy that everything, including the kitchen appliances had to be thrown out. Before they could paint the walls, they had to go around and patch all the gouges and knicks first. She said, Clyde told her it looked like this Browne guy had gone around banging something into the walls. And, she also said, there was all kinds of girly pictures in the place. Did you know him well?”

“No, I didn't, only to say hello if I saw him on the street.”

 **Chapter 17**

The war in Europe ended in victory in April, 1945. Then the allied attention turned to the war in the Pacific. In August, rumors of victory over Japan were circulating everywhere with the news of two huge bombs being dropped over Hiroshima and Nagasaki.

June listened to every news broadcast she could get on the radio. Then, on August 14, President Truman announced Japan's acceptance of the terms of surrender. He went on to say the official V-J day (Victory in Japan) would be September 2, with the formal signing of the surrender terms by

Japan. June put down her knitting, fell to her knees and praised God.

President Truman had not finished speaking when June heard shouting outside. Then fire crackers exploded. Rusty and Vivi came running from their bedroom. "What's happened, Mommie? Why are you crying? Is something wrong?"

"Oh, Rusty, everything is fine. Just wonderful. The war is over!"

"Does that mean Daddy's coming home?"

June hesitated. The ringing of the telephone saved her from answering. It was Hilda. They laughed and cried together.

September turned to October. June waited day after day to hear about Frank. Finally, half-way through October another telegram arrived. Once again June sat in her chair holding the telegram. She wanted desperately to open it but was afraid. She raised a prayer to heaven asking God to undertake with whatever the telegram said. She slid her finger under the opening and pulled out the message. Frank was alive! He was alive! He had been taken prisoner by the Japanese. They had never reported his capture to the Red Cross. He would be coming home. June fell to her knees once again praising God.

Before being discharged from the Army, Frank spent several weeks at Tripler Medical Center Army Base in Honolulu, Hawaii. He was recovering from complications of a gunshot wound. The prison camp had had very poor medical treatment. He was also malnourished and despondent. He knew he didn't have a right to be so low. Many men had returned in much worse condition than him. His problem was a deep-seated hate for the Japanese and how they had changed his life. The physician who treated Frank told him ninety percent of the men he doctored had the same problem. Unfortunately, there was not much treatment given to men with such a problem. They were told to "buck up" and get on with their lives.

The euphoria Frank and June experienced on his return home did not last. His physical health slowly improved, but his emotional wellbeing was stuck in "hate," caused from what he perceived the Japanese had done to him. They were blamed for all the problems he was facing. Many nights were shattered by nightmares as he relived his combat and prisoner of war experiences. Neither was he doing well fitting in at his job as manager of the sales division at R&R.

The older of the two owners of R&R, Ronald, had died in May of 1945. Ronald's son, Harold inherited half of the company. He seemed to always be at loggerheads with his uncle, the other partner, Ralph. They did not agree on how to run the business. Harold wanted to sell his half and often threatened to do so. Ralph would have bought him out if he had had enough funds.

Frank complained about the changes in the department and how Harold, who had avoided the draft, resented Frank's return and was sabotaging his work. Frank believed Harold wanted him to quit. A friend of Harold's had been hired to replace Frank during his time in the Army. When Frank returned and claimed his old position as district manager, Harold's friend was offered a different position at lesser pay.

The friend was furious and quit. He never contacted Harold again.

One evening in May of 1946, at the supper table, Frank was shaking pepper on his potatoes. Six-year-old Rusty innocently spoke up, "Grandpa Grimes puts pepper on everything." Frank pushed his chair back and left the table. Soon June heard the car leave the driveway. Rusty had grown very close to his grandpa during Frank's absence. Rusty had hardly remembered his daddy.

 **Chapter 18**

June sat in her chair facing the cold fireplace crocheting. It was almost midnight when she heard Frank drive into the driveway. She listened to his steps as he came up the walk, unto the porch and opened the door. "June, you're still up! Why? Are you sick?"

"No Frank. I'm fine. We need to talk."

"Talk? About what? What are you crocheting?"

"A baby sweater."

"Oh yeah? Who's having a baby?"

"We are."

"We! Are you…?"

"Yes, We're going to have a baby about Halloween."

He bent over and kissed June. She could smell alcohol on his breath. He sat down in the other chair. They were both facing the cold fireplace. He turned and looked at her, "Well, I hope it's a girl."

"Frank, we really need to talk. We're almost like two strangers, living in the same house. So many couples have divorced. I don't want that to happen to us."

Frank sat gazing at June then bent forward and rested his arms on his knees and lowered his head. In a voice so low June had to lean closer to hear him, he said, "I know June, I know." Then he sat up and glared at her. "It's just that I don't seem to fit in anymore. I feel like I'm not wanted. The only place I feel wanted is with the men who were in the war. They understand."

"Not wanted! How can you say that! I longed for you. I prayed for you to come home."

"But you don't seem to need me around here. Rusty hardly remembers who I am. And Vivian doesn't know me at all."

"Oh, Frank, if only you knew how much we need you. Rusty needs you to be a dad to him. He tells his friends you're a hero. He shows your medals and dog tags to them."

"I'm no hero. The first time I was in combat, I was shot and ended up in a Jap POW camp.

"When I came home, I expected things to be the same as when I left. But things have changed. You are so independent. It's like I'm not needed around here."

"When you left there was no one to help me. I started substitute teaching only because your Army allotment and even with the lease check from the old house, just wasn't enough. I felt so guilty leaving Vivi with your sister on days I substituted.

"You had done all the bill paying, all the yard work, all the home repairs and all the car care. I had to learn how to do a lot of those things. It's not that I wanted to. It was out of necessity. There were times I felt so overwhelmed and tired. I just wasn't sure I could keep going. I'm glad I can turn those things back to you. I'm sorry if it seemed like I didn't want to.

"There was one time I was so afraid. You remember Gaylen Browne."

"That old man that lived next door to Cunninghams?"

"Yes, that man. While you were gone, he started pestering me. He would come over to the house and want in. He stopped me and Rusty one day and insisted we get in the car. He called me up. He even put the children in danger. I was so afraid. Finally, I talked to your folks about him. I don't know what happened, but your dad, Duke and Barney Cunningham went to see him. Right after that Mr. Browne sold his house and moved."

Frank sat up straighter and turned to June, "Why, that dirty rotter! I didn't understand. I'm sorry."

June got up from her chair and knelt on both knees in front of Frank. She took both of his hands in hers and looked into his sad eyes. "Please, share with me what happened to you. I want to help you so much. If you will tell me, maybe I will understand better."

Frank pulled June onto his lap. They sat quietly for a number of minutes. Finally, Frank sighed and began. "I was telling you the truth when I wrote that all I did was fill orders. Our main job was supplying fuel in fifty-five-gallon drums for jeeps and trucks. The day I was shot and captured was just another day. Our orders were to take fuel to a unit about twenty-five miles from our camp. A couple of our guys were taking some wounded men to an aid station. Being short, the captain ordered me to go with the supply trucks. The road was supposed to be secure.

"We were almost to the rendezvous point when we were hit. The road ran along the side of a hill. The Japs attacked us from the high side. We jumped out of the trucks and made for the other side. It turned out to be really steep, almost like a cliff." Frank stopped talking. June knew he was reliving the event.

"Would you like me to get you a drink of water?"

"No, I'm okay." Frank exhaled, leaned back and closed his eyes. Slowly, he continued talking about his capture. "There was a lot of shooting, groaning and cursing. Then everything got quiet. I climbed back over the edge. The guys from my outfit were laying everywhere. Some were still moving. Most were dead.

"Then a Jap came at me. We had an awful fight. It was the first time I had ever been in real hand-to-hand combat like they put us through in boot camp. We were rolling around in the dirt when we both went over the side of the hill. I grabbed hold of a big limb of a tree growing out of the hill. The Jap grabbed a hold of my belt."

Once again Frank stopped and rested his head against her shoulder. June was not sure what to do. She sat quietly praying for Frank.

He finally looked up at June and continued. "I was hanging on for dear life and this Jap was hanging on to me. Then he started climbing, using my body as a ladder. I thought for sure I wasn't going to be able to hold on to that limb or that it was going to break. I looked down. Many feet below was a river rushing over huge boulders. This Nip climbed on my shoulders and pushed hard. I knew he was trying to make me fall." Frank grabbed June's hands so hard, it hurt. "I was saving his life and he was still trying to kill me!" June looked at Frank. She could see the resentment in his eyes.

"Once he was back on the road, I managed to pull myself up. Just as I cleared the edge…he shot me!"

As he finished speaking, he suddenly got up. June slid to the floor. He reached down and picked her up. "I'm sorry Hon. Are you okay? I don't want to hurt you."

"I'm fine." June sat in her own chair and looked up at Frank's forlorn face.

Loud and forcefully, he stated, "I saved that thankless Jap's life and he shot me! That Nip shot me! All those evil dogs are no good."

June stood up and put her arms around Frank. She was afraid he was going to wake up the children. "Please Dear, try to calm down. If you don't want to go on, you don't have to."

"No, now that I've started, I want to finish telling you. You have a right to know."

Taking Frank's hand, June started towards the couch, "Let's sit on the davenport. I think it will be more comfortable."

They sat in the semidarkness produced by the light from a small lamp near her chair. Frank put his arm around June as she leaned on his shoulder. "I must have blacked out for a few minutes. The next thing I knew my friend, Merle Gibson, was trying to get me to stand up. You remember him, don't you?"

"Yes, he's the man from Montana you were always writing about. It made me wonder if you were going to want us to move to Montana, when the war was over."

"I really like that guy. He has such a friendly way about him. He was telling me to get up and walk. The Japs were taking us prisoners. They were shooting anyone who couldn't walk. Right then I hurt so bad I didn't much care if they killed me. He wouldn't let me die. He said I had to live to come home to you and the kids. He lifted me up."

June hugged Frank as tears filled her eyes. She silently prayed a prayer of thanks for Merle helping save Frank.

"We started walking. There were only seven of us left alive. Two other men besides myself were wounded. The four uninjured men were helping us. We walked the rest of the day without stopping. We didn't have anything to eat or drink.

"When it got dark, we finally stopped by a small stream. They let us drink but didn't give us anything to eat. My shoulder was hurting so much I just wanted to quit. Merle tore up his shirt and fixed my shoulder the best he could. He said the bullet had gone all the way through, which was good.

"The next day we again walked for hours with nothing to eat or drink. I stumbled a couple of times, but Merle wouldn't let me fall. The Jap whose life I had saved just looked at me. I suppose he could have shot me again.

"Just before sunset we came to a camp. Once inside we were directed to a hut. It didn't have any sides. Just a rough bamboo and thatch roof.

"Merle helped me lay down on a bamboo shelf. I passed out. When I woke up, my shoulder had been cleaned and bandaged. It was dark and raining.

"Merle was sitting on the bamboo shelf beside me. He had a bowl of rice and some water. He helped me to sit up and fed me. As I ate, he told me one of the Australian prisoners was a doctor and had tended to my shoulder. It still hurt like the dickens. Merle said the doc didn't have any pain medicine.

"The next morning, just as it was getting light, the Japs came in and rousted us out. I could hardly move; I was so sore. We were given some rice, something they called soy and a little water. Every meal, we ever had there, contained rice. Then we were put to work in a quarry.

"It was the same, day after day. The guards were rotten. If they thought a man was working too slow, they would beat him or throw stones at him. Everyday men just dropped dead. Many times, I wanted to give up. I had a picture of you and the kids hidden in my boot. I would get it out at night and look at it. That and Merle were the only things that kept me going."

"I wrote to you almost every day. Did you ever get any of my letters?"

"Honey, we didn't get anything. One day Red Cross packages came. The Japs took all of them. Those lousy Nips really enjoyed sitting and eating our candy bars in front of us."

"How did you know when the war was over?"

"One day some of our men were given some paint and brushes and told by the Japs to go to the top of the permanent buildings and paint "PW" on the rooftops. Then a couple of nights later, we heard a lot of noise in the compound. There wasn't any moon and all the lights were out so it was pitch black. The next morning no guards came to goad us out of bed. We woke up on our own and looked around. All the Japs were gone and the main gate was open. Slowly men started to come out of their huts. There was a lot of talk about what was going on. Most thought it was a trick. They said the sneaky curs were hiding in the jungle and if we left the camp, those sorry excuses for soldiers would shoot us."

"We helped ourselves to what little food the deserters had missed and just laid around. About four in the afternoon a small plane with U.S. insignia flew over. The pilot dipped his wings to let us know he had seen us, then left. Just before dark of the same day, a Flying Fortress came over. The bomb bay doors opened and out came a bunch of leaflets. They said the war was over and we were to stay in the camp. Help was on the way.

"You can't imagine the joy. Grown men shouting and crying. Some got down on their knees and thanked God, right out loud. All the misery was finally over. Some of the guys had been prisoners for three years or more. I was a relative newcomer, only a few months."

"How long was it before you got help?"

"The next day a Super Fortress came over and again the bomb bay doors opened. Canisters came out. Some of the men thought they were bombs and said it was a trick and we were all going to be killed. But the canisters broke open when they hit the ground and inside were all kinds of food, clothes and medicine.

"It kept happening every couple of days.

Then on October second... a day I'll never forget. On that day, through the gate came truck after truck, each with a white star! They were U.S. Army trucks, six by sixes. Eventually we were taken to an aid station. And you know the rest, hospital, travel, discharge and I got home soon after that."

June leaned into Frank, resting her head on his chest. She kissed him lightly on his neck. Frank sighed. He paused reflecting, "This talk was difficult for both of us. Thanks for listening to me."

They sat quietly wrapped in each other's arms. Finally, Frank got up, walked to the lamp, and switched it off. He returned to the couch, picked up June and carried her to the bedroom.

Chapter 19

The following Sunday, Frank went to church with his family. June was so pleased. Rusty had begun to complain about going when his daddy stayed home. During the service he sat beside Frank. June could see the pride on both their faces as they sat side-by-side.

After the service Frank and Ben Walker stood talking in the narthex. The new pastor walked up to them. "Good morning, gentlemen. "I'm Rev. Haas, the new pastor." The three shook hands. "I'm so glad you've come today. I've been wanting to meet you." They talked for a short time about lighthearted things. Finally, Rev. Haas came to his point.

"I know both of you served in the war. Ben didn't you have two ships shot out from under you?"

"Pastor, yes, I did. I got two new seabags but lost a lot of buddies." The three men stood silent.

Rev. Haas broke the silence, "Frank you were a Jap POW, weren't you?"

"That's right."

"I'll be honest with you two. I landed in Europe on D Day. I spent the next twelve months holding men's hands and praying as I watched them die. When I returned to the states, I erroneously thought that would be all behind me." He pointed to his head and continued, "It's still all here. I can't just pick up where I left off and go on."

Frank and Ben looked at the pastor in disbelief. Neither had any words to say.

"So, I've been doing a lot of praying. I'm hoping what I am about to suggest, will be a help to you and to me. I want to start a war vets' Bible study group. The study would be directed towards our needs. Besides studying a Bible lesson, it would be an opportunity for the men to discuss problems we're having. Perhaps by sounding off and sharing our problems we can help each other. Think about it. When I get things ready, I'll put a notice in the church bulletin. Please understand, I don't have all the answers. I'm struggling just like a lot of other guys.

The meetings were held on Thursday evenings at the parsonage. Only three men came to the first meeting, Rev. Haas, Frank, and Ben. The next week, five men attended. After four months the attendance fluctuated between eight and fifteen. Some of the men attending were not even parishioners of the church. Frank seldom missed a meeting, although he spoke very little to June or anyone else about what was discussed. He really respected Rev. Haas and what he was doing.

Rusty and Vivi were getting too old to be sharing the same room. And with another baby due, June and Frank knew they needed more room. Frank suggested they move to a larger house. June loved the stone house and did not want to leave it. They agreed to hire a contractor to discuss adding on to the cottage.

June was uncomfortable as the contractor,

Fred Miller, walked about, taking notes. She did not want the look of the front of the house changed. Finally, Fred, June and Frank sat down at the kitchen table. Fred showed them two possibilities. June rejected the first one out of hand. It would totally change the street-side view. She accepted the second proposal.

The addition would be a shed dormer across the back of the house. Fortunately, the house was strong enough to accommodate a second floor. The present bathroom would be replaced with a turn-about stairway. The children's bedroom would become the downstairs bathroom and utility room. In the upstairs Fred suggested a bathroom and two large bedrooms or three small ones. June thought three smaller ones would be better. It would give each of the children their own space. Frank chirped up, "What if there's a fourth or even a fifth baby?" June frowned at him.

June loved the idea of a first-floor utility room. She remembered, only too well, carrying laundry up and down the basement stairs while pregnant.

The contractor was ready to start the project as soon as the final plans were drawn and the finances were arranged. Frank insisted the utility room be done first. He did not want June lugging laundry baskets up and down the stairs. June was touched by Frank's concern for her wellbeing.

In preparation for the remodeling project, the dining room furniture was moved to the garage. Rusty's and Vivi's beds and dressers were moved to the dining room. June bought a second-hand screen at a thrift shop to put between the dining and living rooms. The children thought it was like camping out, only long term.

 **Chapter 20**

"Well, June you sure did it this time." It was October 14, 1946. June had just given birth to her second son. "Where did that boy get all that red hair? It looks like we'd better call him Danny Boy."

June smiled as she lay in the hospital bed. "My mother's father, my grandpa was born in Ireland. He had the most beautiful red hair. My grandma said it was a shame it was wasted on a man."

"What was his name?"

"Liam O'Connor."

"How 'bout Danny Boy Liam."

June laughed, "Don't you think Daniel Liam would be better? We can always nick-name him Danny Boy."

June thought Frank was conquering his war time memories. Although he occasionally had episodes of depression and an infrequent nightmare. He started attending church fairly regularly. He had even been persuaded to be part of the ushering crew. On volunteer workdays he enjoyed working with the other men. Everyone spoke well of him. June was aware, however, that he never gave witness of having accepted Christ.

Another major concern of June's was Frank's working situation. He continued to complain about the men with whom he worked. The young owner, Harold, frequently carried on about how he managed to avoid the draft. This peeved Frank to distraction. Most of the younger men had not been in the service. Some had very liberal and unpatriotic opinions. One out-right told Frank he had been a fool for allowing himself to be drafted. June quietly listened to Frank's frequent complaints.

One evening June served a rice dish for supper. When Frank saw it, he picked up the serving bowl with the rice and threw it out the door. Turning to June he said, "Don't ever serve rice in this house again."

Rusty and Vivi sat wide eyed watching the episode. Nine-year-old, Rusty looked at his dad and asked, "Can I throw out the food I don't like?"

Frank stood at the door glaring at Rusty, "Only if you've been in a war. Then you can eat or not eat whatever you want. As a matter-of-fact, I told myself while in that rotten, steaming jungle whenever I wanted some ice cream, I was going to get some. And right now, I feel like an ice cream cone. So come on. We'll walk to the Schneider's place and have some ice cream." June never again served rice in any form.

Once Danny Boy started talking, he never stopped. His grandmother Grimes said Danny Boy had a switch attached from his eyes to his mouth. In the morning when he opened his eyes, it turned on his mouth.

One Sunday in church when Danny Boy was about three, June was having a terrible time keeping him quiet. Finally, Frank picked him up to take him to the vestibule for a serious talk. When they were about half way out, Danny Boy shouted for all to hear, "When I grow up, I'm going to be a preacher so I can talk in church."

Seven-year-old Vivi and her special friend,

Agnes loved to sidewalk roller skate. The sidewalks had been constructed just after World War I. There were many cracks in them. One day the two girls were having a grand time skating until Vivi fell. Her arm hurt terribly, worse than she could ever remember it having hurt in her whole life! June heard her crying half a block away as she sorrowfully walked home holding her right arm against her body. Agnes followed carrying both pairs of skates. Wanda Miller a registered nurse, lived just to the north of the Grimes. She also heard Vivi and came out to see about all the noise. After looking at the arm, she was sure it was broken.

That night Frank came home to see Vivi sitting in his chair with her plastered arm in a sling. Learning the facts and after consoling Vivi he asked, "Where are the skates?" When told they were by the back door, he picked them up and tossed them into the trash bin. This distressed Vivi even more than she already was, and flabbergasted June.

Two summers later Vivi and several friends were playing a game called 'Statue'. In this game a person would twirl another person around holding on to only one hand. When let go the person who was being twirled would 'freeze' in whatever position he or she landed. Once when Vivi was being twirled she landed on her left arm which broke. Frank forbade the children to ever play the game again. Rusty was irate. He really enjoyed swinging the girls around.

Another activity Rusty enjoyed even more than playing Statue was riding his bike. Some summer days he would leave the house right after breakfast and not return until almost supper time. He liked to ride over to his grandpa's house. Grandpa usually had a project going and let Rusty help.

Frank seemed to have lost the bond he had with Rusty and Vivi. They were very attached to their grandparents. This bothered June, but she was at a loss as how to help. When Danny Boy was five, he had a book about fishing. He asked to be read this story, over and over. Then he started pestering his parents to go fishing. Frank remembered going fishing with his friends at the local stream that ran along the east side of town. It was contaminated now and 'No swimming or fishing' signs were posted along the bank. He thought, "What fun we boys had."

One day after reading the book to Danny Boy and listening to him whine once again, about going fishing, Frank finally gave in. "Okay, okay this Saturday we'll go fishing!"

Frank went to Jackson's Rental Supply and rented five poles and other equipment he would need. Friday night he watered an area of the backyard. When 'night crawlers' came to the surface, he had the children come out and pick up the worms putting them in an empty coffee can. Vivi protested, "This wasn't my idea. I don't want to go fishing!"

"Too bad. Do as I say. You may find that you like fishing." Frank chuckled to himself.

The banging of a spoon on a pot lid awakened the children at 6:00 the next morning. Three doors opened and a sleepy head popped out of each one. "Up and at 'em. Times a waste'n and the fish are waiting." Frank continued to bang on the lid as each door closed. He laughed as he went down the stairs.

As things turned out, Vivi did find, she

enjoyed fishing. However, she refused to bait the hook. Danny Boy had no qualms about putting a worm on a hook. He happily baited his sister's line.

Rusty found that he did not really care to fish. He would rather go hunting with his grandpa. This hurt Frank. He never said anything to his father about his feelings. Instead, he focused setting aside time to fish with Vivi and Danny Boy. June saw what was happening. After spending time in prayer, she decided to let God handle the situation.

One day Rusty was riding down the lane from the road to his grandparent's house. His cousins Milo and Everett were also visiting their grandparents. They now had a six-year-old sister, Leah. She was standing in the middle of the lane. Rusty was traveling fast and yelled at Leah to get out of the way. Frightened, she stepped right in Rusty's path. He hit her hard. He jumped off the bike and ran to her. She lay very still. Rusty was sure she was dead.

The adults were sitting on the porch and saw the accident. By the time they reached Leah she had regained consciousness and was crying. Grandpa Grimes said that was a good sign. Ruth, Leah's mother after examining her daughter, didn't think there was any broken bones. Grandpa got his car and drove Ruth holding a still crying Leah to the hospital. She was kept overnight and released the next day.

Rusty really felt bad. He followed his mother's example and prayed all that day, not only for Leah but also that his dad wouldn't toss his bicycle in the trash. Frank was quite philosophical about the whole thing. He said, "A six-year-old kid shouldn't have been out there by herself." Then he gave Rusty a stern look, "And young man, you be more careful."

The summer of 1952 was a grand time for the Grimes's family. It was their first ever vacation. Frank had just bought a new Chevrolet station wagon. He and June decided to take a trip to Montana to visit Merle and his family. Frank's father Art Grimes had died earlier that year. June invited her mother-in-law, Hilda, to go with them.

The family had a wonderful time at the Gibson ranch. The children ran about unrestricted with the Gibson children, four girls. They made all the noise they wanted and no one yelled at them to be quiet. Rusty's favorite activity was riding a pony accompanied by his dad and "Uncle Merle." One evening Rusty returned from a day of riding. On his hip was a six shooter. "Look, Mom, Uncle Merle showed me how to shoot. And I killed a rattle snake! I'm not scared of snakes anymore, as long as I have a gun."

June's reaction was, "Well, my story about the snakes in the vacant lot kept him alive until now."

To reassure June, Merle looked at Rusty and said, "And remember all the gun safety, I told you about."

In the evenings, after supper the two families would gather around a camp fire as Merle and his wife, Eleanor, delighted the children with stories about the early days in Montana. Both of their families had come to Montana from Texas in the 1880's to claim free land. Merle told of his grandmother, Doris, running from outlaws. Eleanor interrupted Merle to add her grandfather had taught Doris to shoot a gun. And later Doris had shot an outlaw.[1]

The Gibson girls sat bored as they listened, yet again, to the same stories they had been hearing their whole lives. Rusty, however, was mesmerized. The camp fire danced in his eyes as he imagined himself a cowboy fighting outlaws. He decided right then, at the age of thirteen, to one day return to Montana. He would become a rancher and marry one of the Gibson girls, he was not sure yet, which one.

Roberta was the eldest, two years older than Rusty and rather bossy. He did not think much of her. Then there were the twins, Shelby and Cindy. They were his age. Shelby was pretty nice. She smiled a lot. Rusty liked that. Cindy was quieter

---

1   **Secret Circumstance**

and mousy. Either one was a possibility. Virginia was the youngest. She was the same age as Danny. A lot of families seemed to have children with a big age gap between the youngest and the next older. Rusty had not quite figured out why that was.

Chapter 21

Polio was the scourge of children living in the decades of the forties and fifties. Each summer thousands of children, mostly under the age of fifteen, were contracting the dreaded disease. The summer of 1956, had been a particularly trying time. The Fairview swimming pool had been closed all summer, causing ire among the children and the relief of mothers. Some Vacation Bible Schools were cancelled as were summer camps.

In July, Allen Bancroft, age six and his brother Raymond, four, had been diagnosed with the disease. They lived across the street from the Grimes. Vivi had been a regular baby sitter for the boys all summer while the parents worked.

June prayed exceedingly hard for both the boys, their parents and for her own children. If ten-year-old, Danny Boy complained of his legs hurting after playing all day, she feared he was getting polio. Grandma Grimes would say, "It's just growing pains." Now with the end of summer near, mothers hoped the worst was over.

It was! Jubilant news swept across the town. The newly developed Polio Vaccine would be administered by the County Health Department. Clinics were scheduled at several locations. Children ages fourteen and under were eligible to receive the life-saving serum. While in church the Sunday after the notice, June and many other parents thanked God for answer to their prayers.

Most children had no reaction to the shot. Danny Boy sat at the dinner table holding a bag of ice on his left arm. He had received his shot for polio earlier that day. The rest of the family sat around the kitchen table finishing supper.

Seventeen-year-old Rusty, a senior in high school, could not stop talking about the football team. He played wide receiver because he was tall and had a knack for catching the ball. Two-a-day practices had already started for the team. He was the first-string right end. He was sure the team had a good chance of winning the state championship.

Vivi, fourteen, had received her polio immunization with no adverse effects. She didn't openly say anything, but she was concerned about Rusty. Because he was seventeen, he was not eligible to be vaccinated. Vivi tried to make light of the situation. "Boy, is my arm sore. Rusty you're sure lucky you didn't have to get jabbed. I hope this doesn't interfere with my cheerleading practice."

Vivi was trying out for the cheerleading squad. She had tried out last year as a freshman and did not make the squad. She and her new best friend, Georgia had practiced cheers all summer. Both had high hopes of making the squad this year.

June noticed Frank had not eaten much. "Frank, you've hardly touched your supper. Don't you like it?"

"Oh, nothing's wrong with the meal." He hesitated before saying anything more. Slowly he looked at each of his children, then at June. To none of them in particular he said, "How would you like to move to Fremont?"

All four spoke at once, "Dad, this is my senior year. I can't move to Fremont! It's at least a hundred miles from here."

"Me neither. I'm going to be a cheerleader."

"Where's Fremont?"

"Quiet, children. Why do you think we should move to Fremont?"

"I don't think we should move there. But that's where my job is going to be." All eyes were on Frank, as he continued, "You know Harold, the half owner in the company? Ever since his father died, he has wanted to sell out. Well, Midlands Grocery Supply Corporation has made an offer, too good for Harold and his uncle Ralph, the other owner, to pass up. Midlands is buying R&R. They have a large operation in Fremont.

They'll get our customers. But most of the work at R&R is just redundant of what they are already doing. So, they're closing the operation here and moving everything to Fremont. The buildings here will be used only for storage. If I want to keep my job, we'll have to move."

Once again Rusty protested. "Well, I'll just go and live with Grandma. She'll let me stay here and finish my senior year. Vivi, I bet she'll let you stay here too. After all she has a great big house and she's the only one living in it."

"No one is going to go live with anyone. You children go to your rooms or go watch television. Dad and I need to talk about this. Vivi, before you go, please put the leftovers in the refrigerator. Frank let's drink our coffee on the terrace."

Frank and June walked out the screen door

as the children left the table. Vivi took her time clearing the dishes trying to listen to her parents conversation.

"I'm sorry. I should have told you first."

"What's done is done. How long do you have to decide? Do you really want to stay with the company and move to Fremont?

"No, I don't want to move. But I have to have work. There have been rumors floating around for a couple of months. We were told the buy-out papers were signed this morning. They've given me three weeks to let them know if I plan to move with the new owners. I've worked my tail off for that company since 1934. This is the thanks I get."

"You haven't been happy with your job since returning from the war. How many times have you threatened to quit? Maybe this is the right time to find something else."

"Actually, I've been thinking about that too. A couple of days ago Ray Rademacher happened to call me. He and his dad own the car dealership where we bought our car. He heard about the company's possible moving. His dad is retiring. He said he'll be needing someone to work in the office. I'm not sure exactly what all I'd be doing. But it wouldn't be selling cars. He said if I'm interested to come in and see him."

"I don't think Ray just 'happened' to call you. I think God led him to place the call. And I think you should talk to him about the job."

"You and God! Sure, I'll see him. I wish I had your faith."

The following week Frank took Tuesday morning off to talk to Ray Rademacher. June received a telephone call at the very time the two men were meeting. The call was from Miss Cantrell, the new school superintendent. "Hello, Mrs. Grimes. I hope I've not called you at a bad time."

June's first thought was that there was some problem with one of the children's school records. She ran each child quickly through her mind but could not come up with anything. "No, Miss Cantrell but, this is a surprise. How can I help you?"

"I'll be frank. I know you were not treated well by us when you originally came to teach in thirty-eight. However, you did substitute during the war. I also know you've renewed your teaching certificate every year."

"Yes, it's like an insurance policy. One

never knows what might happen. I enjoyed teaching. Why is that of interest to you?"

"You know there has been a tremendous increase in the number of children since the war ended. I'm sure, you are also aware, we are opening a new school this fall, in just two weeks. We are in desperate need of teachers. I still have openings for kindergarten, second, fifth and sixth grade teachers. Have you ever considered returning to teaching? I promise we will treat you better than we did last time. You can have your pick of which grade you want to teach and you will be paid for your years of experience."

June thought the superintendent sounded like she was going to start crying. "Miss Cantrell, this is a big decision. I couldn't possibly give you an answer on the spur of the moment. I'll think about it, talk to my husband, and also pray about it before I let you know."

That evening Frank came home looking more depressed than he had in a long time. June could tell things had not gone well at the job interview. "What happened? Didn't you like the position Ray offered you?"

"Oh, I liked the job offer just fine. However, Ray offered me much less than I'm making now. I just don't see how we could get by on such a pay cut."

June thought about telling Frank about Miss Cantrell's call. She hesitated. She feared in his tenuous emotional state he would feel she thought him inadequate.

"June, I know you and the kids don't want to move. Truthfully, I don't either. We really have a nice place here. And we need to think about Mom. I don't want you to think

I'm not able to care for my family. But, if I take this job, how would you feel about going back to teaching? Maybe it would only be for a few years. Maybe just until Rusty gets out of college."

June smiled at her husband. "I told you last week nothing just happens. God has a plan for each of us." She then told Frank about Miss Cantrell's offer.

When June talked to Miss Cantrell, she requested to teach the second grade. It had been quite a number of years since June had been in a classroom full-time. The first year was very difficult. She was so proud of how her family pitched in to help. Frank took over the laundry, Rusty kept the floors clean and Vivi cleaned up the kitchen after meals. Danny Boy now in the fifth grade, came to her classroom after school. He helped decorate the room for each holiday, washed the blackboards and occasionally helped check test papers.

The high school football team was not the state champion in Rusty's senior year. However, they did have a winning season. Vivi cheered them on as part of the cheerleading squad.

June and Frank were surprised when Rusty came home from school in February of his senior year and said he wanted to enlist in one of the military services. June wasn't sure how to respond. "I thought you were going to go to college in Montana and be a cowboy?"

"Mom, I still want to. But if I enlist in one of the services, the government will help pay for college when I get out. What do you think Dad?"

"If you're really intending to join, I'd rather

you enlisted in the Navy. They have better food and clean sheets."

June put her hands on her hips and said, "Frank! I don't think that's a good reason for enlisting."

Rusty laughed then said, "I heard the Navy has what's called a "Minority Cruise." If I enlist before I'm eighteen, I will be out on my twenty-first birthday."

After more discussion and talks with a recruiter, Frank and June signed a permission form for Rusty to enlist in the Navy. Two weeks after graduating from high school he left for Navy boot camp at the Great Lakes Training Center, Chicago, Illinois.

 **Chapter 22**

In April of 1965, as June walked home from school, she was thinking about the changes that had occurred over the twenty-seven years of her marriage. She passed the Frazil's house. By the porch step sat a rather sad looking yard ornament. It was made of discarded plates and bowls that had been glued together. On the top sat a ceramic bird with one wing missing. June noticed that the bird's beak was also only partly there. The ornament had been a Girl Scout project. Trudy Frazil had been in the same troop as Vivi. June had volunteered as an assistant leader for six years. She wondered what had become of Trudy. Trudy had dropped out of school at sixteen and run away. No one ever heard from her again.

June walked on and noted the Bancroft's home across the street. The family still lived there. Both Allen and Raymond had done well recovering from polio. Raymond still wore leg braces. June knew Allen was in the high school band.

Her mind drifted back to Ella and her son Eddie. June had made a commitment to herself, to write to Eddie once a week. She kept him up-to-date on the news in Fairview. She knew, he couldn't read or write; someone had to read her letters to him. Occasionally she sent him pictures of her children and candy bars.

Eddie's sister, Mildred still managed the Painted Porch. Her mother and Aunt Stella were retired and lived in a small house not far from June. Ella's desire to see Eddie was so strong that at the age of forty-eight she learned to drive. She bought a car and visited him regularly. After the war a new interstate highway had been built which made the trip easier.

Rusty never forgot his dream of returning to Montana. In the fall of 1960, he was discharged from the Navy and entered Montana State University majoring in farm and ranch management. He had much to learn. Merle Gibson took Rusty under his wing and mentored him. He treated Rusty like the son, he never had.

Rusty worked school-breaks and summers at the Gibson ranch. In 1961, between his freshman and sophomore years he married Merle's older twin daughter, Shelby. June, Frank, fourteen-year-old, Danny Boy and Hilda made a second trip to Montana.

Vivi had been in the last trimester of pregnancy. Her physician advised against traveling. He thought she might be carrying twins. Vivi and her husband, Jim Fletcher, went to Sears Roebuck and Co.® and bought all their baby furniture and layette. Sears' policy was, if a couple had bought their baby needs from them and had twins, the store would give them a free set of all they had bought.

June's parents, Charles and Della Witherspoon opted to fly to Billings, Montana. They rented a car and driver to take them the rest of the way to the Gibson ranch.

It had been a grand reunion. The wedding was held in a small country church. Shelby was beautiful in a gown she had made. June thought how perfect the couple looked together. She prayed they would have a long and happy marriage.

Frank had been very quiet during the wedding and throughout the reception. June stole a glance at her husband as they sat watching the wedding couple cut their cake. He appeared to have tears in his eyes. Yet he looked peaceful. He felt her looking at him. Turning to her he said, "I am so happy. Just think, Merle and I are now related!"

Rusty graduated three years later in 1964. Frank and June flew to the graduation. Vivi and Danny Boy opted to stay home. Frank and June stayed in Montana for two weeks. They helped Rusty, Shelby and her parents remodel a home on land owned by Rusty. June and Frank had loaned money to the couple to help buy the acreage. Frank said the money was a graduation gift. However, Rusty insisted Frank and June's name be included on the deed until he could pay them back. He continued to work at the Gibson ranch learning, 'how to be a rancher.'

That same year Mabel Cunningham passed away. How June missed her. They had been friends since before the Grimes had moved into the stone house. Now Barney Cunningham lived alone. He and Frank were still friends. June made it a point to have Barney over for dinner at least once a week.

Vivian had married her high school sweetheart the year after she graduated. They had moved several miles from Fairview and were now the parents of twin boys. Vivian's husband and her father-in-law had opened a fast-food fried chicken franchise. The business was very popular.

Vivian came in to work on days when extra help was needed.

Danny Boy graduated from high school a year earlier than his classmates. He enrolled in a church college and began studying to be a minister so he could talk in church! Just three more years and Danny Boy, or Rev. Daniel Liam Grimes would be a minister with a church probably miles from home.

June gazed at her lovely stone dream house. It seemed so empty with all the children gone. Then she noticed their car in the driveway. What was Frank doing home so early? She quickened her pace.

Frank was not in the living room. "Frank, where are you?"

"In here."

June dropped her school valise and

hurried into the kitchen. Frank sat at the table drinking a cup of coffee. All kinds of fears rushed through June's mind. Had something happened to one of the children or grandchildren? Was it Hilda? She looked into Frank's eyes and knew it was something bad. Slowly she sat down. "What is it, Frank? What's wrong?"

Frank sat gazing at June for what seemed an eternity. Finally, angrily, he sighed, "I've been fired."

"Fired! Why? I don't understand. You've been with Rademacher's twelve years. Ray always spoke so well of you. What could have happened that you would be fired?"

"The dealership is closing. Remember about five years ago that German auto dealer opened a place just across from Schneider's Ice Cream Emporium? It seemed all the people in town were buying those tiny bugs. Next that Jap dealer opened down by the Baskerville Funeral Home and took a bunch of our business.

"We would have been better off losing the war. Instead of us rebuilding their factories and us continuing to use hundred-year-old plants, those scheming defeated soldiers could have come over here and rebuilt our factories. Then they would still be using their old factories."

June gave a long-exasperated sigh. She had been hearing such comments for so many years.

"Anyway, Ray is closing the business. He'll be sixty-five in a couple of months. He plans to retire and move to Florida. Meanwhile, what am I to do? There doesn't seem to be anybody that wants to buy an American car dealership. Who's going to hire an old, broken-down, ex-GI who helped save his country? Maybe I should just sit around the house and let my wife support me."

June sat stunned. She did not know what to say. She could not think. She did not even know how to pray. Suddenly, Frank pushed his chair away from the table and got up. "I'm going for a walk."

June continued to sit for several minutes. Then she slowly knelt down and bowed her head by Frank's chair. "God, please, please, do something. Undertake for Frank's good. I don't care what it takes. I'll do anything. I'll give up anything. Just help Frank. I love him so and I know You love him too. Please, please, I pray in Jesus's name."

 **Chapter 23**

For a while, things continued normally. Nothing more was said about the situation. June continued to teach. During her lunch breaks she stayed in her room. But instead of eating, she prayed and fasted, begging God for help. Frank continued to work at the dealership.

One day as June was praying, she felt a sweet, reassuring peace. God whispered in her mind, "Trust me, Child. I'm still in control." There was joy in her heart. She gave the situation to God.

Soon after that, one evening just after ten

p.m., Frank got home after being gone all evening. "June, you know the Radcliffs and the Walkers?"

"Well, hello to you too."

"Sorry Hon. It's just that I have something important to tell you. It's an idea Jack Radcliff, Ben Walker and I have." Frank, Jack, and Ben had all gone to high school in the same class. The three men had served in the war. Jack was single and volunteered the day after the bombing of Pearl Harbor. He had seen service in Europe. Ben like Frank had been drafted. Fairview was a small town and as the war continued more and more older men were being called up. Ben was a yeoman in the Navy. He had been on two ships that were sunk from under him.

"Look at this brochure." He handed a tri-folded, high-gloss pamphlet to June. She saw it was an advertisement for an old banana plantation in a South American country, Costa Mesa. She handed the pamphlet back to Frank and looked at him with trepidation.

"The three of us think we should buy this place. We figure we can make it into a ritzy resort. It's the going thing now. There are a bunch of places along the coast. This will be the only one inland."

June could hardly believe what she was hearing. Before she could gather her thoughts to voice any doubts to the idea, a small voice whispered inside her head, **"You said, 'whatever it takes.'"**

She took the brochure from Frank and looked at it more closely. It showed a beautiful two-story white building with red shutters. There was a picture of a lovely flower garden amidst manicured lawns.

Another picture was a view of the sun shining on a deep blue lake. Smiling and with a confident air she really did not feel, June spoke, "Tell me about your plans."

Frank sat down in his chair and leaned forward towards June. "Well, it seems people are looking for more exotic vacations than just a trip to the beach. The main building would have several single rooms we can rent out, plus a lounge, dining room and of course a couple of offices and living quarters for us. There are old slave quarters on the grounds. These could be remodeled into small cottages for guests. How does it sound so far?"

"I'm sure there are possibilities, as you say. But I think we need to slowly and meticulously think this through. It's an awfully big commitment. To say nothing of the change it will mean in our lives."

"This place is a real bargain. It won't last long. You know 'catch the tide at the right time' or something like that?"

"Yes, but what about the children?"

"The kids! We see Rusty once or twice a year. We'll tell him to come down with his wife for a vacation. As for Vivian, if we didn't drive out to her place once in a while, we'd never see her. She can also bring her family down for a vacation."

"What about Danny's schooling? We have to have money available for his tuition."

"We will. We will. We still own the property with the warehouse, out at the edge of town. I heard a new housing development is planned for the area. I bet we can get a really good price for the land. And by selling this house…"

"Sell our home!"

"Sure, it's too big for the two of us even if we were to stay here. What do we need with four bedrooms?"

"Where would we live?"

"At the resort. When we come back for a visit, we can rent a place to stay."

"What about your mother?"

"Mom is living with Ruth. She'll be just fine. She may even want to come down to live with us, once we get the place fixed up. Please, June, I really want to do this. I know we can make it work."

June had not seen Frank so excited and happy since Danny's birth. "Well, I need time to think it over and pray about it."

"Sure, there's a meeting planned for tomorrow night. I hope it's okay, I told the guys we could meet here. They're bringing their wives with them."

Jack and his wife, Imogen arrived a bit early the next evening. June served coffee as the four waited for the Walkers. They were almost an hour late. June got out of her seat, "Would anyone like their coffee warmed up?"

Jack offered his cup to June. "You can warm mine up. What do you suppose is keeping Ben? He's known for punctuality." Growing up, Jack and Frank were often taken for brothers. They had the same color of brown hair and brown eyes. Their complexions were similar as were their heights. The similarity ended in their looks. Jack was an easy-going and fun-loving man. Frank had always been quiet and reserved. Whenever there was a good time to be had, Jack was sure to be nearby and often trying to pull Frank and Ben along with him. Nothing seemed to upset or discourage him.

"Imogen, would you like a refill?" Imogen and Jack had married late in life. She had been thirty-two and he was thirty-six. They were married on a whim a mere three days before Jack shipped out. When he returned, they realized, they had little in common. Their marriage was one of convenience.

Imogen had lived with her parents before her marriage. She continued to live with them while Jack was gone. Before her marriage, she had acquiesced to her parents demands. When Jack returned, she deferred to him.

Imogen had a sad looking face caused by a drooping mouth. She was short, solid, shy, and backward. The one thing that had attracted Jack was her gorgeous Hollywood figure. She had been a perfect hour glass. During his absence he believed all she must have done was eat. Somehow all the sand in the hour glass had sunk to her hips.

"I'll have a little more if there's enough. But, don't make anymore, just for me."

June smiled at Imogen, "There's plenty."

Frank grabbed June's skirt as she passed him, "Here Sugar Cakes, fill mine." He pinched her leg which caused her to splash some coffee on the carpet. "What's a girl like you doing working in a joint like this, anyway?" He was so energized and upbeat.

June smirked at Frank just as the doorbell rang. Frank stood and started for the door, calling over his shoulder, "That must be them now." He walked to the door.

"Ben, come in. What took you so long? Where's Sharon?"

Frank stood aside to let Ben enter. He stood by the door looking sad and miserable. He habitually complained that Fate had used a marked deck of cards against him. Ben accepted his lot, as life unraveled around him.

June took one look at Ben and knew something was wrong. "Come in Ben. Let me get you a cup of coffee. I hope Sharon isn't ill."

"Thanks June, but that's not necessary. I won't be staying."

All eyes were on Ben. Finally, he said, "Me and Sharon's been talking about this resort business. She's been having some medical problems. You know she's got the sugar. That's the disease where you can't eat sweets."

"Do you mean diabetes?"

"Yeah, that's it." Well, it's been acting up lately. She thinks maybe it has something to do with this resort business. You know, we'd hate to get down there and have her get real sick or something."

"Ben, I'm sorry about Sharon, but there are doctors in Costa Mesa. It's not Timbuktu." June could see fear on Frank's face as he uttered his concern.

"I know Frank. But we've decided to pull out of the deal. I'm sorry. I know this is going to make it tough on you. But we have to do what we think is best for us. I'm really sorry. I love Sharon and I have to do what's best for her." Ben turned to leave.

Jack stood up and glared at Ben, "Just a

minute Ben. You can't just waltz in here and suddenly change your mind, just like that."

"Darling, Ben and Sharon have to do what they think is right. We'd do it if the situation were reversed." To everyone's surprise Imogen had spoken. Jack turned and frowned at his wife as she fell silent. She looked as if she wished she could melt into the sofa.

Frank took hold of Ben's arm, "Ben, what about the money you've already put up?" This bit of information was news to June. She did not know their plans were so far along. "You can't expect us just to fork it over. We need it."

"I don't know. I won't lie to you; we really would like the money back." All was silent for several seconds. "How about we call it an interest free loan? Once the resort starts to show a profit, you can pay it back, a little at a time. Would that be agreeable?"

June looked at her husband, "That sounds fair to me. Don't you think so?"

To no one's surprise, Imogen stated, "I'll agree to whatever Jack decides is best." Frank rolled his eyes at Imogen, to which June gave him 'the look.'

Frank turned to Jack, "Well, I guess it'll have to do, if you agree."

"I guess so." Scowling at Ben he added, "But, don't expect the pay back any time soon."

As Ben turned to leave, he apologized one more time, "Thanks, and again I'm real sorry. I wish you success. I think I would have enjoyed the venture. I've never done anything like that".

June walked over to Ben and put her arm around his shoulders, "You and Sharon are still our friends. Tell her to call me anytime."

"Thanks."

As June returned to go to the kitchen, she noticed Jack trying to inconspicuously place a small pill under his tongue.

 **Chapter 24**

The stone house sold quickly to a young couple with two small children. The couple had actually been June's former students. Dinah, the woman buying the house, her mother and June were already friends. They had visited each other often. Dinah had jokingly said, on a number of occasions, she would love to buy the cozy stone house, if June ever wanted to sell it.

The morning of the closing, June walked one last time through the rooms. Most of the furniture had been given away. Only a few things such as her sewing machine, were in storage waiting to be shipped.

June loved this house. She remembered the first time she had seen it. Her mind raced through all the memories, the Christmases, the birthdays, the happy suppers, the anxious months waiting to learn if she was a widow. "Oh God, I know I said I would do whatever was necessary for Frank to find peace. But I never thought it would cost so much. Help me to understand that this house and our possessions, are just things. Please, help me to let them go." Just then the wind picked up and she could barely hear the sweet, soft sound of the guitar strings. She was glad they had never repaired the window.

Vivian, her husband, Jim Fletcher, and the twins, Darrin and Derick were at the airport to see June and Frank off. Frank was euphoric at finally leaving. June tried to contain her sorrow. Vivian was distraught and searched for a handkerchief to wipe her tears. "Mother, please don't go. I've never been without you. I already miss you."

June did her best to comfort Vivian while trying to maintain her own composure. "Sweetheart, it won't be so bad. You can come for visits and we'll be back now and then. I think it will help us to be more appreciative of each other."

The boarding was announced. Everybody hugged and kissed. "Say, where are the Radcliffs? Shouldn't they be here?" Jim, Vivian's husband, said this as he looked around.

Frank gave each twin one last hug, "They'll be coming in a couple of weeks. Jack has to have some medical tests first."

Vivian alarmingly looked at her mother,

"I hope it's nothing serious. I don't like the idea of the two of you being alone so far away."

Her husband chuckled, "For Pete's sake, Vivian, they're grownups!"

Vivian waved her handkerchief, sobbing as her parents walked out the door across the tarmac and up the steps to the waiting airplane.

It had been a long tiring trip. They arrived in the late afternoon at the small town of San Marza. No "swanky" resorts were in evidence. The town was more of a "back water" hovel. To their chagrin, they learned while the country may have originally been settled by the British, most of the present inhabitants spoke Spanish. Only a few knew any English.

"Are you by chance looking for a taxi,

señor?" Frank turned to view a dark, slightly built, curly-mustachioed man of about forty. "By chance are you the Americanos who have purchased the banana farm?" He spoke in broken English with a heavy accent.

"Yes, we are. Do you have a taxi? Can you take us there?"

"Sì, Señor, my name is Carlos Abrego. I am a very quick, but good driver."

Carlos was true to his word. The road to the plantation was dirt, rutted and narrow. Each side of the road was thick with tropical vegetation. The road wandered up and down and around hills of various sizes. Carlos drove as though he were in a race. It was twilight when the taxi pulled into the driveway.

Frank and June happily got out of the car

then stood aghast in the yard. Their faces fell. Turning to Carlos, Frank asked, "Are you sure this is the right place?" He began searching through his carry-on for the brochure. "We expected a large plantation house. This house is little more than a shack. In fact, it's a dump!"

"Sì, Señor, this is the correct address. It is not such a good plantation. There used to be a bigger house, but it blew down, three months ago, during the last hurricane season." Gesturing to the smaller house still standing Carlos continued, "The overseer lived in this house."

"You're kidding! No, you're not! Well, that's just great! We've been flimflammed. The three stood looking at a two-story house. The first floor was made of adobe brick. The second story was white-washed wood. A number of the window shutters hung precariously from rusty hinges. The front door was gone. A few tropical flowers were fighting a losing battle with weeds around the base of the house.

June contemplated the house in depressing incredulity. What had they gotten themselves into? Her first notion was to get in the cab, return to the airport and fly home.

"Where are the workers' houses? There's supposed to be a bunch of little houses that went with this shanty," uttered Frank.

"They're still here! They're behind the big house, around by the lake. I'll show you."

June knew Frank and she were not going to quit and return home. "Let's take our things in the house first. I want to see the inside."

The inside was as bad as she expected

it to be. The floor was so dirty she could not tell what kind of covering it had. She moved the tip of her foot back and forth over the dirt hopeful there was something under it. Most of the windows were broken. The stair banister to the second floor was missing.

They walked through a bare second room into a third. It contained a small table, two chairs and a very small open doorless cupboard. "Is this the dining room?"

"No, Señora. This is the kitchen."

"Where is the sink? And what is that awful smell?"

Following the smell, they walked out a door to a veranda. June looked in horror at a mud hole where several pigs rooted. Trying to sit down in a wooden lounge chair, it collapsed under her weight. She sat in the pile of broken wood and started to cry. Frank hurried to her and took her in his arms.

"Please don't cry, Darling. I'm sorry. I didn't know it would be like this. The agency said the place only needed a little fixing up." She straightened her dress, looked up at her husband and smiled. Frank asked, "Are you hurt?" June shook her head.

June was thinking, "This is how I started out my married life. I certainly didn't expect to end it like this." She would be brave. June turned to the taxi driver, "Carlos, where is the lake?"

"You are looking at it, Señora. It gets bigger in the rainy season."

"Whose pigs are those? Are they wild?"

"Oh no Señora. They belong to the Vasquez family. They live in the first house over there." Carlos pointed to a row of small houses as he was talking.

Frank spoke up, "What do you mean, live in the first house? Isn't that one of our cottages? Isn't that on our property?"

"Sì Señor. But, for a long time no one has lived here. Señor Vasquez needed some place for his family to live and the house was empty…"

"Okay, okay, but he's got to move, and so will anybody else that is living here."

"But, where will they go?"

June came to Carlos's and the Vasquez's defense. "It will be all right for them to stay for now. We have a lot of work to do on the "big" house."

Frank turned and started walking back into the house, "We'll have to see about that.

Right now, I'm bushed. Let's see if we can fix this place up enough to cook a meal and get some sleep."

"Señor, there is no electricity or running water."

Carlos helped them buy a surprisingly good truck. After visiting the electricity company, four days in a row, Frank was finally able to get the electricity turned on. They now had running water of sorts. There was a large holding tank outside the back door. Once a week Frank purchased water in town to fill this tank. To use it for drinking or cooking it still had to be boiled.

Over the next several weeks, Frank and June worked like slaves themselves to get the adobe house in a modicum of order. They quickly got to know the people living in the little houses and in the area.

Lola Vasquez and her husband, Fidel, were particularly good workers. Lola helped June clean the flooring. Under the dirt was beautiful terrazzo. It took a lot of time and elbow grease. When the two women were done, the floor glowed. Lola continued to help clean the kitchen. Lola taught June to make local dishes using available produce. This was an unexpected bonus. She compiled a book of recipes to use when there were paying guest at the resort. New commercial appliances were ordered. They were not expected for several weeks.

Fidel worked with Frank building a banister. Frank had never done carpentry. Fidel's father was an experienced carpenter. Fidel had learned much working with him. Together Fidel and Frank repaired the shutters and replaced broken window glass. Frank was enjoying learning these new skills.

Paint had been ordered, but had not yet arrived. That seemed to be the story with most orders. Frank wondered how the economy kept going when everything you wanted had to be ordered and seemingly never arrived.

Frank had not quite figured out how many Vasquez children there were. The oldest boy, Andres, became a 'go 'fer' boy for Frank and Fidel. Frank wasn't sure about his age or why he wasn't in school, but he was a good worker like his dad.

June resented her present situation. She disliked the heat and humidity. She thought, "Who in their right mind would want to spend time in a place like this?" She constantly thought about her beautiful stone house. She missed her daughter and grandchildren. She prayed incessantly,

"Lord, help me to have faith for what I cannot see."

Frank came into the kitchen as June was finishing the morning dishes. "I'm going into town to get the mail. And there are some things I need to pick up at what passes for the hardware store. Is there anything you need? Or do you want to go with me?"

"Sure, I'll go. Just give me a minute to finish here. You know I can't figure out what's taking Jack and Imogen so long to get here. You'd think they'd dropped off the face of the earth. They haven't even written. I have a feeling something's terribly wrong."

"I agree. I wish they'd get here. How about we send them a telegram?"

"What a good idea! I hope Imogen gets to

like this place. Of course, that'll depend on Jack!" June chuckled at what she'd said, before continuing, "It's probably worked out better that we came first and got this house livable. Is that a car driving up?"

A car door slammed as they walked to the front of the house. Carlos came running up the path. "Señor, Señora! You have a telephone call at the police station. Come! Come quickly, please!"

"We were getting ready to come to town. Carlos, I'll drive the truck and we can follow you." Carlos ran back to his car, turned it around, and drove hastily down the dusty road followed by the Grimes in their truck. Just before entering the town, Frank hit a chicken but kept going.

June sat beside her husband as she twisted her handkerchief in her hands, "Oh, I hope nothing has happened to one of the children or grandchildren." Frank looked at June's worried face. He could think of no reassuring reply.

At the police station Frank was told to dial the zero and ask for operator number three. Several policemen milled around watching. After what seemed like an eternity, Frank reached his party. He said very little, only, "Yes, no, but, yes, I understand. I'm very sorry." He hung up the phone and looked at June, "That was Imogen. Jack's dead...heart attack!"

June slumped onto a bench. The chief-of-police poured water from a jug and handed the glass to her. She smiled at him as she accepted his kindness. Frank sat down beside her. June passed the glass to him. He took it but only held it. "He was my oldest friend. I've known him since...since the first grade. That's over fifty years. I can't believe it. I just can't believe it. He's dead! I won't even be there for his funeral. Jack's dead, June. Dead!

June looked at Frank's cloudy eyes. She realized he was holding back tears. Putting her arm around Frank, they sat quietly for several minutes. Finally, she got up and led him out of the building, thanking the chief as they left. She whispered in Frank's ear, "Come on, let's go home."

Chapter 25

Danny Boy sat at his desk studying for mid-term exams. He had been studying most of the day. He was hungry and was struggling to stay awake. He shared the room with two roommates. A Japanese young man, Koki Yonai, was one. The other roommate was from a Polish family now living in Chicago.

When Frank had learned, a Japanese was going to room with Danny, he blew his top. He tried to get Danny's room changed. The administration told him the request for change had to be made by either Danny or Koki. Danny told his dad he did not want to change. He liked the idea of having a "foreigner" as a roommate and he liked Koki as a friend.

Koki's family had immigrated to the United States when he was twelve. His father managed a company owned by the young man's grandfather, who still lived in Japan. The family was apparently very well-to-do. Koki was a likeable enough person, although he had a trace of arrogance. He had learned to guard his actions because secretly he felt just a bit superior to Americans.

Ron Andrew was the third roommate. He was very tall, several inches over six feet. His gorgeous curly blond hair was the envy of all the girls. Blue eyes sparkled under long lashes. Ron told his roommates the original family name had been Andrzejewski. The officials on Ellis Island had changed the name to Andrew when his grandfather had immigrated in 1905 from Poland. For all his good looks he was still a lanky, uncoordinated, twenty-year-old. He started college late, not really caring about attending college. But he did not like working either. His dad told him, to either get a job, attend college or join the Army. Ron was friendly, but could be obnoxious and a bit much to take in large doses.

The door opened. Ron entered flopping onto his bed and rolled onto his back, "Hey, guys, what's up?"

Danny turned and held up a book, "Midterm exams, Dunce-brain." He turned back to his desk and continued to study his notes.

"Ha, I don't believe in studying for exams. I figure if yeah don't know it by now, yeah never will."

Koki who was laying on his back, rested his book on his chest and looked at Ron, "Ron, you don't believe in studying, period!"

"Well, I listen real good in class."

Koki turned back to his book, "You mean with your eyes shut. And in your dreams!"

"Enough of this. I didn't come in to get bad-mouthed. What I really want to know is, do you guys have any plans for spring break? I was thinking about going to Florida."

Giving up trying to study, Koki slammed his book shut, "I'll probably just go home for the week."

In singsong voices both Danny and Ron replied, "BORING!"

Then Danny jumped up and in an excited voice said, "I have a terrific idea. How would you two like to spend a week in a tropical paradise?"

Ron looked suspiciously at Danny, "Do you mean the ex-slave camp your parents have in Brazil?"

"It's not in Brazil. It's in Costa Mesa. And it's a swanky resort! I'm sure my sister will spring for my ticket, so I can go check up on my mom and dad. She worries about them like they were her children."

Ron sat up and put his thumb nail between his middle teeth trying to pick out something, before saying, "How much are we talking? I can probably hit my dad up for the money, as long as I get it before he finds out my grades."

Danny turned to Koki, "What about you Koki? Can you get the money to go?"

"Who! Mr. Money Bags!" Ron said mockingly.

Koki ignored Ron, "Sure, I can go. It sounds like fun. Count me in."

Throwing a phone book at Ron, Danny muttered, "Here, look up a travel agent and find out how much the tickets cost and whatever else we need to know."

Ron picked up the phone book and thumbed through it. "Pharmacies, refrigeration, towing, trash, aha! Travel. Year-Round Fun Travel Agency, airline tickets, cruise specialists, vacation planning, group travel, no service charge. Sounds like what we're looking for!"

After dialing the number and waiting for several seconds, his roommates were startled when Ron stated in a most dignified voice, "Good afternoon Jennifer.

This is Mr. Ron Andrew. I'm in need of information to…" Ron put his hand over the receiver, "What's the name of the place again?"

 **Chapter 26**

June stood on the veranda waving two letters in her hand. Frank was a distance away working on one of the cottages. Three little girls playing with their dolls nearby called "Buenos días," to June.

June was slowly learning the language. She smiled at the children repeating, "Buenos días, niñas". The children giggled at June's pronunciation.

"Frank, Frank! I have a letter from Imogen."

Frank hearing June's call dropped the shovel he was using and hurried to the veranda. "Have you read it? What's it say?"

"No, I haven't opened it. Carlos just brought it. Let's sit down at the table. I'll get you a drink of water. You look like you need one."

Frank took the letter from June as she went into the kitchen to get each of them a glass of water. He sat down and tore the envelope open. June returned and sat across from Frank. "What does it say?" He read the letter out loud:

"Dear friends,

I've tried to write this letter four times now. What can I say? I still can't believe Jack is gone. I keep waiting for him to come in from the garage or garden. I catch myself setting a place for him at the table. It's just terrible."

June murmured, "Oh, poor Imogen." Frank paused, looked at his wife, then continued.

"But I must get to the point. I'm sure you're wondering what I am going to do as far as the resort is concerned. As you know, Jack did all the family business. I depended on him, so much. I'm so thankful for the help of my family. I doubt if I could have survived these last weeks if it weren't for them, especially my sister Ann and her husband Gerald. I'm not sure you ever met them. He's a lawyer. He has been so good to take care of all the finances and paper work. I've tried to tell him as much as I can remember about the resort agreement between us. So much of it was just talk. I guess I should have paid more attention to what you and Jack were doing.

Whoever would have thought something like this would happen! Anyway, Gerald has all the papers I could locate about

the resort deal. He's looking them over. I really don't have any head for business so I'll just have to do what he thinks is best.

Oh, how I wish you could have been here for the funeral. I'll keep in touch and let you know what's happening at my end.

Sincerely, Imogen"

Frank put down the letter. The two stared at each other. Finally, June spoke, "Poor, poor Imogen. I feel so sorry for her. She's right about never making a decision. I can remember how exasperated I would get with her sometimes. She wouldn't even buy a dress without showing it to Jack first. She would always ask the clerk to hold it for her until she could bring Jack in to look at it.

"I feel so sorry for her. I can remember when I thought you might be dead. I felt so adrift. I wish we were there to help comfort her.

"Frank, what will we do if she pulls out?"

"We'll be finished. That would be it. We'd lose everything." Frank got up from his chair and began to pace. His glass of water remained untouched. "Lawyers! That woman never has and never could make a decision on her own! She just can't pull out now. Her son-in-law has to see how much she'll lose if she backs out now. She just can't."

Frank sat back down and picked up his glass. He looked at June as he raised his glass to his mouth, and took a drink before setting it down. "Isn't there another letter? Not more bad news, I hope."

"I hardly think so. It's from Danny." June opened the letter and began reading:

"Dear Mom and Dad,

I'm coming down to visit you during spring break. Vivi gave me money for the airplane ticket. My two roommates are coming with me. We arrive March 16, flight 257, 3:48 p.m.

I can't wait to see you. You haven't told me much about the resort. Can hardly wait to see it. I hope it has a pool. Have you started having paying guests yet? If the rooms are all taken, we can sleep anywhere. I know it's going to be fun.

Love, Danny"

"Isn't it wonderful! Oh, I can hardly wait to see him. Frank, what's the matter?"

"What's so wonderful? He's just coming

down! And bringing two others. I seem to have missed the part where he asks if it's okay to come and bring others with him. What if we already had something planned for March 16th?"

June got out of her chair and went over to Frank putting her arm around his shoulders. "Frank, stop talking like that. You know you'll be glad to see Danny. He's your old fishing buddy."

Frank pulled June to his lap, "Oh, June, I'm such a failure. I'm sorry you have such a lousy husband. I'm sorry you've had to put up with me."

"What are you talking about? We've had a wonderful life together. I've never regretted marrying you. I love you so much. I wouldn't want any other life."

They kissed. The little girls watching them started to giggle.

Chapter 27

Danny came running down the outdoor portable ramp used by the Costa Mesa airport followed by his two roommates. "There he is! Danny! Danny!" June waved her handkerchief wildly in the air as she called to him. Danny ran over to his mother, picked her up and swung her around. June breathlessly told him, "Put me down!" After Danny released her, she said, "It's so good to see you. Did you have a good flight? You're even bigger than the last time I saw you."

"Mom, you say that every time! Hi Dad." Danny with one arm around his mom, offered his hand to his dad. "You remember my roommates, Koki and Ron?"

June glanced quickly at Frank than looked at the young men, "Hello, welcome to Costa Mesa." Both smiled and nodded to June.

Koki offered his hand to Frank, "Hello Mr. Grimes. I hope our coming won't be a burden on you."

Frank had not said a word. He had a scowl on his face, though, he did shake hands with Koki and Ron. "Well, let's get your suitcases and get on home. I hope you didn't bring much. We don't have much room in the truck. You boys will have to ride in the back of the truck with your luggage."

They arrived at the resort and unloaded the boys' bags. The boys stood by the truck and stared. "Dad this doesn't look much like a fancy resort. What happened to the beautiful landscaping shown in the brochure? I thought the lodge was larger? Where is the swimming pool?"

"Ha! You should have seen it when we first got here. I'll tell you about it later. Right now, I'm hungry."

June had hired Lola Vasquez to prepare a local dish of fish and rice. Frank was learning to tolerate rice since it was a prominent food source in this country. The group sat down at the table.

Danny spoke up, "Boy Dad, you sure have been quiet. Aren't you feeling good or somethin'?"

"I'm fine. Just fine."

"How do you like retirement, Mr. Grimes?

My grandfather in Japan did not wish to retire. He feels working keeps him vibrant."

"I'M NOT RE…"

"You should hear about Koki's family." Ron spoke up before Frank could continue. June could not decide if he grasped the potential gravity of the moment or was just impolite.

"They lived in Nagasaki and, before the bomb, were real rich. Then BAM!" He slammed his palm onto the table causing the cups and saucers to jump, as did everyone. "Just like that, they were dirt poor, penniless. But, tell them what your family did, Koki."

Koki stood up and bowed. "My family's home was Nagasaki, where the second atomic bomb was dropped. Fortunately, the day before the bomb was dropped, my grandparents had left the city to visit relatives. They watched from the mountains and could see the cloud from the bomb. They came back to find all their possessions were gone and their daughter, husband and two grandchildren dead.

My father was in the war, as you were Mr. Grimes. He was captured just as you were, only by the British and spent two and a half years in a prison camp." With a mild smirk Koki continued, "He came back hating both the British and the Americans."

Frank continued to look as though he wanted to beat someone up. Danny knew how his father felt about the Japanese and recognized his father's discomfort, "Hey, come on, lighten up. We're here for a vacation. Let's drop the economics and politics. It sounds too much like school. I'm hungry. Koki can say grace."

Scowling at Koki, Frank muttered, "Who yeah pray to? One of your Shinto gods?"

"No sir. I pray to the Lord Jesus Christ."

"To Jesus! He's an American God, not one of your Jap gods."

June was incensed, "Frank!"

Smiling Koki replied, "That's alright Mrs. Grimes. Mr. Grimes's surprise is to be expected." Koki turned to face Frank. "Mr. Grimes, Jesus is the One True God for all people. Not just Americans. Not all that happened during the war turned out bad. May I tell you how my family became Christians?"

"Sure, but…June say a prayer so we can eat."

After everyone was done eating Ron spoke

up, "Go on with your story, Koki. It's really interesting."

Hesitantly, Koki looked at Frank. When Frank did not say anything, he continued. "Grandfather had nothing, but he did not give up. He worked very hard fifteen-twenty hours every day. Soon he had established a small but good business. It grew due to our family's hard work. When I was twelve, he acquired a business in the United States that had gone bankrupt because of poor management and employee greed.

"My parents and I came to the U.S. My grandfather chose to stay in Japan. My father is now managing the U.S. business. It is worth well over a million dollars."

Ron stood up and put his arm around Koki, "Koki says Japan couldn't defeat us with physical strength, but, if we're not careful, someday they'll defeat us with economic strength because we're so lazy."

"You said your family is Christian. How did that happen?" This was asked by June.

Koki continued talking about his family. "One day, in 1946, an American missionary came into my grandfather's establishment to ask directions. He began talking in Japanese. This impressed my grandfather very much. The missionary left that day but returned several days later. He continued to visit the store for several weeks, actually making purchases.

"He gave Grandfather a New Testament Bible written in Japanese. At first Grandfather didn't want to read it and put the Bible away. Then one day, when business was slow, he remembered the book. He hunted through various drawers until he finally found it. He began reading it and was curious.

The next time the missionary came in, Grandfather had many questions. They started meeting early in the morning before Grandfather opened for business. One day they were discussing John 3:16. The missionary said that God so loved the world that He gave His only begotten Son, that WHOSOEVER believes in Him should not perish but have everlasting life.

"Grandfather wasn't sure this meant Japanese people. Maybe it was only for Americans. The missionary said WHOSOEVER meant even Japanese people. That day Grandfather accepted the Gift of eternal life."

June stopped Koki. "Let me clear some of the dishes and get coffee and dessert before you finish your story."

The group sat around the table drinking coffee and eating a local dessert June had brought with them from a bakery in town. Koki continued his story. "I would like to tell you about my Grandmother. She was very upset when Grandfather told her about becoming a Christian. She didn't want to go to church with him. But Grandfather made her go. Being a good Japanese wife, she obeyed. She told me, to her surprise, she really liked the church, especially the singing. After attending several times, she also became a Christian.

"My father was twenty-seven when my grandparents became Christians. He hated the Americans and wanted nothing to do with their God. He resented my grandparents' conversion. They did not pressure him. They just prayed, mightily. They got him to go with them one Sunday. Playing the piano was a very lovely girl.

He went back each Sunday just to see this girl. He asked her out several times. She always said no. She instead, gave Father a copy of **Pilgrim's Progress**. He didn't really want to read it. However, it was in English, and he had been trying to learn English. So, he decided to read it just to practice his English.

"He read about Pilgrim's difficult journey. He came to the part about Pilgrim coming to the cross and laying his burden down.

"One week the church had a wonderful revival. The visiting evangelist preached about giving Jesus one's anger and hate. He invited anyone who wanted to, to come to the altar and trade his burden of sin for Jesus's peace. My father went forward and accepted Christ. The next time he asked the piano player for a date, she accepted. Two months later they were married and

Christmas day of 1948, I was born." Koki gave a big smile. "And my father doesn't hate Americans or British anymore."

June also smiled, "What a wonderful legacy you have. So, your mother was from a Christian home?"

Koki swallowed a bite of dessert before continuing. "My mother's story is quite different. One day when she was fourteen, some people gave her a New Testament. Her mother caught her reading it and threw it away. Later, she got it out of the trash bin and continued to read it secretly. She said it had such nice stories; she couldn't understand why her mother would forbid her to read it." Having said this, Koki paused to take a sip of his coffee. Everyone sat staring at him.

"She wanted to go to the Christian church but was afraid to. However, her desire was so great, she went whenever she could. She said her father would often beat her for attending. They even had a Shinto priest come to talk to her.

"One day she came home and told her parents she had accepted Jesus as her Savior and would no longer take part in ancestral worship with them. Her father was so angry he beat her very badly and made her leave home.

"She was taken in by a Christian family and worked for them as a baby sitter and house keeper. Her parents, my grandparents, have never spoken to her since that day. She has tried to contact them many times, but they have refused to see her. I've never met my maternal grandparents. Mother has often quoted Psalm 27:10, 'When my father and my mother forsake me, then the Lord will take me up.'"

Frank pushed back from the table and got up. Sarcastically he uttered, "Well, isn't that just a wonderful story." There were several seconds of uncomfortable silence.

Breaking the silence, June spoke. "Say, I have an idea. Frank, how about a camping trip? You know, we've been working so hard, ever since we've come here. A few days off will do the two of us good. Why don't we rent some camping equipment and do some sightseeing? We really haven't seen much of the country at all. We'll need to be able to tell people what there is to do and see here. That is, once we start having paying guests. How would you boys like to explore the jungle?"

Ron got up and roared, "ME TARZAN! Where's Jane?"

Chapter 28

Frank was restless and unable to sleep. He quietly got out of bed and walked to a window, staring into the blackness. To Frank's surprise June spoke, "Frank what's the matter? Please, come back to bed."

"You just don't understand. That Jap kid, I've just…just had an awful feeling come over me. Why did he have to room with Danny? Why did Danny bring him down here? Doesn't Danny understand how I feel?

"Seeing that young Nip brought back so many angry memories and harsh feelings. Things I've forgotten so long ago and feelings I didn't even realize I had anymore."

June climbed out of bed and went to stand beside Frank. "What do you mean about feelings you didn't realize you had anymore?"

"I resent his grandfather being such a success. The company he bought in the States could be the place I worked. He could be the reason I lost my job. And the war, June, the war!"

"The war? It was twenty years ago!"

"I know, and that's what I don't understand. All day I've been remembering so many things, so long forgotten. So many friends died, like Mark, my friend from high school. I feel like such a failure, almost a coward for staying alive when he and others died."

June leaned into Frank and put her arms around him. "You're not a coward. You did what you were ordered to do. You did what you had to do. Your death wouldn't have saved any of those men. Please, come to bed."

"All right. Just give me a minute." Frank continued to stare out the window. June reluctantly returned to bed and prayed until she sensed Frank getting into bed beside her.

June packed boxes of items for the trip while the men drove into town to rent camping equipment. She was ready when they returned. After a quick mid-morning snack, June and Frank got into the truck cab. Frank had secured a plank across the box of the truck behind the rear window. The boys sat facing backwards on the plank.

After a couple of hour's drive, deeper into the jungle, Frank drove to a clearing about one-hundred feet off the road and stopped. He got out of the truck and looked around. "This looks like a good place to set up camp." He had given orders to each of the boys. He and Danny started setting up the tent. "Where are the stakes? They should have been here with the tent. Danny, go see if they're in the truck bed."

"Steaks? Wouldn't they be in the ice chest with the rest of the food?"

"Not steaks to eat! Poles to hold up the tent. The rental man gave them to you, didn't he? You know, when we picked up the rest of the equipment this morning?"

"Aaah, I don't remember seeing any stakes. What are they supposed to look like? Ron, Koki, did either of you pick up any stakes?"

"Well, I saw something like long sticks or poles beside the tent on the counter. I didn't know we were supposed to bring them with us." Sheepishly, Ron continued, "I just left them there."

With his hands on his hips, Frank glared at Ron. "Great! Just great!"

Danny came to Ron's defense, "Well, c'mon, Dad, how were we supposed to know? None of us has ever been camping before."

Frank walked over to a tree about eight feet tall and chopped it down with a machete he kept stored under the seat of the truck. Then he stripped off the limbs. "See this? Go find three more just like it, and eight smaller ones about three feet long each. AND BE SURE TO WATCH OUT FOR SNAKES!" Frank smirked as the three young men prudently started foraging for suitable trees and limbs to be used for tent poles.

"Frank, you are treating those boys like little children. You're making me, them and yourself miserable."

Frank made two fists, bending his arms and shaking his elbows in the air replied, "Well, I am miserable! I feel…..all bound up."

Softly, to herself, June uttered, "Oh, heavens, I hope I remembered to pack some mineral oil."

That evening after supper June heated water preparing to wash dishes. Frank walked over to her, "Hold it June. You fixed a mighty nice supper. You boys, get over here and do up these dishes."

Koki looked horror-stricken, "Wash dishes! That's women's work. I've never done dishes!"

Frank very gently put his hand on Koki's forearm and propelled him to the wash basin. "Well, there's a first time for everything. It won't hurt you to learn." Frank continued as the two stood in front of the basin, "Pick up the dish rag. Stick it inside the cup, swish it around. Pull it out. Wipe around the outside. Now hand it to Ron."

While saying this, Frank motioned for Ron and Danny to come over. Koki handed the tin cup to Ron, "Now Ron, put the cup in the rinse water, then hand it to Danny. Danny take the towel and wipe the cup the same way I just explained to Koki only using the towel. There you are, boys. You have one cup done. Keep it up and at this rate, when you're finished, you'll be ready to start on the breakfast dishes."

The boys continued to wash the dishes.

Frank put another log on the fire and June stepped into the tent. She came out almost immediately. "Has anyone noticed all the traffic there seems to be on the road?"

Koki stopped with his hands in the dish water. Ron held a fork that he had just rinsed in mid-air. Both father and son turned to look in the direction of the road which was shielded by a rise between the campers and the road.

Cynically, Frank said, "Well, it's Friday. Maybe the locals are going home to a wedding or something for the weekend." June gave Frank an exasperated look and went back into the tent.

The fire burned low as the campers were sleeping. That is, the four men slept. The increase in traffic did not seem to bother them. June lay listening trying to hear above the snoring. Something unusual was going on. Besides the noise of the occasional automobile and truck, she could hear people walking, and carts being pulled by horses with muffled hooves.

June was the first one up the next morning. She'd had very little sleep. She walked over the rise to see the road. Startled by what she saw, she hurried back to the tent and woke up Frank. "Frank, get up!"

He was instantly awake. "What is it? What's wrong?"

"Come with me to see for yourself." The two walked over the rise. They saw a procession of people, a few cars, trucks, and carts heading for the mountains.

Taking June's hand, Frank started down the other side of the embankment, "Let's go down to the road and see if we can find out what's going on."

They tried asking several people what was happening. No one paid them any attention. Finally, Frank grabbed a man by the arm and tried to talk to him in English. The man shrugged off Frank's hold and continued walking. June tried talking Spanish to a woman. The woman looked at her confused and continued on her way.

A young boy of about twelve stopped. In halting English, he told them, "You have not heard? The president is dead. General de la Cruz has taken power. We are heading for the mountains for safety. It is not safe in the cities. There is much shooting and..." Before he could finish his mother grabbed him and led him away.

Frank took June's arm. "Come on. Let's get packed up and get out of here. We'll go to the little town we passed on our way up here and see if we can get more information about this coup."

Frank was driving the truck with extreme vigilance. There continued to be people walking, carts being pulled, and a few motor vehicles chugging along, all moving in the opposite direction. They finally arrived in the village of Lucinda just before noon. Greeting them was a multitude of people in considerable bewilderment. It seemed some were walking in aimless confusion. Others, with more presence of mind, moved with purposeful bearing. Very prominent was a conglomeration of various military vehicles. Some of the vehicles looked fresh off an assembly line. Others looked as though they could be relics from the First World War. One was even being pulled by donkeys.

A goodly number of military men loitered about, most seemingly having no purpose. Frank noticed a man dressed in what could pass for an officer's uniform. Frank parked the truck on a less crowded side street. Getting out of the truck he turned to the boys, "Don't move, stay right where you are."

He walked back to where he had seen the officer. "Excuse me, Sir. Do you speak English?"

"A-ha, a Norteamericano! Yes, I speak a little English. You are no doubt on your way to San Marie Harbor?

"San Marie? No, why would we go there? It's at least a hundred miles southeast of here. We live in San Marza. We just want to know what in the world is going on."

"Then, my friend, you have not heard?"

"Heard what?"

"Alas, our dear president has met with an untimely, and not-at-all unexpected death. Our valiant five-star general, General de la Cruz has declared himself president. Unfortunately, the general does not care much for you foreigners. Now, I myself, have nothing against you. As a matter-of-fact, I have a sister and brother-in-law in the United States, Cleveland. But I am but a lowly captain, and orders are orders."

"What orders?"

"In three days, we have been ordered to shoot all aliens who are still in our dear country."

"What are you talking about? We live here. I own a house and property in San Marza!"

"I do not think you own a house any longer. As I said, I like Norteamericanos, but…"

"I heard you, I heard you, the general doesn't. So, what are we supposed to do?"

"As I said. Go to San Marie Harbor. In three days one of your Americano Navy ships will be there to get you. General de la Cruz is not totally unkind. He is giving all gringos three days to get out of his… our country.

"After that, if I see you, my orders are to shoot you. Please do not take it personally. I myself like Norteamericanos. One day I hope to maybe join my sister in your United States, Cleveland. Please do not try to go back to San Marza. Take my advice and leave now for San Marie. The road here to your right will take you directly there. Do not turn off at any point."

Frank stood speechless. He was having difficulty grasping what he had just heard.

"Please, Mister, I do not want to shoot you. Go back to your truck and family and leave for San Marie."

Frank turned on his heels and hurried back to the truck. Everyone started asking him questions at the same time. He held up his hands for silence. June and the three boys sat flabbergasted as Frank repeated the information.

Ron was the first to speak. "Shoot, me?"

Danny looked at his dad with marked alarm and asked, "He's kidding, right? This is all a joke. It has to be."

Koki began to pray. June looked at him and said, "Koki, say a prayer for all of us."

Frank got in the truck and started driving, yelling at the boys in the back, "Watch for a gas station."

 **Chapter 29**

The road, if it could be called a road, to San Marie was in terrible condition. It was rutted, little more than a wagon path. At least there were not as many people on this road. Frank drove as fast as he dared. They had only gone about twenty-five miles when they came to a roadblock. Several men, not in uniform, were obstructing the road, each man armed with a machete. Frank stopped the truck.

A man speaking in Spanish told them to get out of the truck. The armed men, by motioning, made them understand to get out.

Ron started howling, "Oh, great, just great. What do we do now? We're all going to be shot!"

"Ron, shut-up." Frank had had about all he could take. He did not need a bawling kid adding to the problem.

To the surprise of everyone, the men only got in the truck and drove away, leaving Frank and the others standing in the road. Frank started walking. The rest continued to stand in the middle of the road. "Come on, start walking. We've already gone about twenty-five miles. In three days, we should be able to walk the other seventy-five."

Once again, Ron expressed his displeasure, "Wonderful. That's only twenty-five miles a day with no food or water. And would you believe? I can't remember one word from my two years of high school Spanish."

June walked beside Frank. She looked at him and uttered, "I wonder if the three-day period started today. Or does it start tomorrow? Or maybe it started yesterday, since it's when the coup d'état happened."

"Thanks Mom, thanks. That's just what we needed to hear."

The weary travelers had been walking for about four hours. They rounded a bend and saw their truck turned over and smashed into a tree. The hijackers lay in disarray around the truck. Frank told the others to wait where they were. He walked to the site and checked each man's blood-stained body. All were dead. Frank motioned for the rest to come forward.

"Wow! What do you suppose happened here? Do you think they were going too fast and wrecked?"

Mockingly, Danny answered Ron, "Duh, Ron, what do you think? Do you suppose the tree branches made all those holes in them? Duh!"

June looked troublingly at Frank. "Do you think the general's soldiers did this? Would they really do this to us?"

"Who knows? Let's look over what's left. See if there's anything useful, a canteen of water or anything else. Then, just to be on the safe side, we'll walk single file close to the side of the road. If you hear anything or anyone coming, head for cover behind the brush."

Several knives were liberated from the fallen men. Koki tried getting a knife out of its sheath from one of the men. His hands got blood on them and he threw up.

Most of the food June had prepared for

their camping trip had been eaten by the hijackers or taken by whomever kill the men. Some camping equipment such as blankets and cooking utensils were found. Each took a dead man's ruck sack and filled it with the items they had acquired. Frank took one last look around before stating, "That seems to be it. We'd best get going."

The group continued down the road. Ron turned around for a moment and reviewed the scene one last time. "Is that what the war was like, Mr. Grimes?"

"Worse."

It was near sundown. The travelers were very tired and haggard looking. The road had gotten noticeably more overgrown with jungle vegetation. It was getting difficult to keep on the road as darkness approached.

"Man, am I ever hungry!" complained Ron.

"And thirsty!" added Koki.

"Dad, how much longer are we going to walk before we rest? I don't think I can go on much further."

"You can't go on? YOU CAN'T GO ON? You're not even twenty yet. What about your poor mother?"

"Please, don't worry about me. I…" June dropped to a pillow of grass. From not getting much sleep the night before, all that had happened today and walking so much, if the truth be told, she felt almost exhausted. The rest of the group followed her lead and found spots to rest. Suddenly June perked up, "Is that running water I hear?"

All listened without moving or even breathing hard. "It's over in that direction," pointed Frank as he got up and helped June up. They started walking deeper into the coppice of trees.

The others hurriedly followed Frank and June through the brush and found a small brook. They all flopped down on their stomachs for a drink. The water was clear and very cold.

Danny lifted his head after satisfying his thirst, "Hey, look, there's fish in this creek."

Frank waded into the cold water, "I think we just found supper. June start a fire. Just a small one and try not to make too much smoke. We don't want to attract anyone's attention. You boys get in the water with me."

"Mom, how are you going to start a fire with no matches?"

"I wasn't a Girl Scout leader for five years

without learning a few things. You don't think Boy Scouts are the only ones that know how to survive in the wild, do you?" June proceeded to gather twigs and within minutes had a small fire going.

"I was a Boy Scout for six years and never mastered that," uttered Danny as he waded into the cold stream.

The boys stood around Frank wondering what they were supposed to do. Frank interlaced his fingers in the water and stood perfectly still. Soon a fish swam between his hands. In one swift motion, Frank closed his hands around the fish and tossed it onto the creek bank.

"Where ever did you learn that?"

"Koki, this is exactly how we Allied prisoners managed to stay alive, when I was in a Japanese prison camp. There was a small stream running along behind the camp. At night we took turns sneaking out to fish." Frank stood up, "In all honesty, I think the Japs knew what we were doing and just turned a blind eye, as long as we came back. It helped us to have more to eat than what little they provided. So enough talking. Get busy and catch your supper." The cold water felt good on the boys' feet.

"I got one! I got one!" No sooner had Ron expressed his joy when he lost his grip on the fish. He chased it along as it slipped from one hand to the other. Then he tripped and with a big splash fell into the water face first. As the water settled around him, he raised an arm into the air firmly holding the fish. "Boy, this water sure is cold!"

Frank's next job was to show the boys how

to scale and clean fish. Danny had grown up fishing with his dad and knew what to do. Frank and Danny had gone fishing often. It was the one activity that had helped Frank bond with Danny.

At first, Koki thought of refusing to scale the fish, then thought again. He picked up a knife and went to work. Ron was just glad to have something to eat. June cooked the fish. It tasted good after a day with no food.

Before nightfall they reluctantly quenched the fire. Everyone knew it was too dangerous to chance strangers seeing it in the dark. A night chill set in. Even though each person had a blanket liberated from the truck, they slept close together to conserve heat.

Frank got up before dawn. He entered the cold water and began throwing fish onto the side of the creek. June was awakened by what she at first thought was a cold rag hitting her. She opened her eyes to see a large silver and gray speckled fish flopping near her head. "Sorry Hon," Frank said with a sheepish grin. "I wasn't trying to hit you."

Frank came out of the water and began gently rousting the three boys with his bare foot. "Up, and at 'em, men. Get up NOW! Time to be greeting the day. If you want breakfast, go catch it."

Chapter 30

Just as the sun began to penetrate the jungle foliage the little troupe of refugees were once again on their way to San Marie. They had been walking about an hour when the sound of a vehicle was heard coming towards them. Koki was walking on the opposite side of the others. He scampered into the jungle on that side. The others sprinted for cover on the near side.

Watching from their hiding place, they saw a jeep come into view and stop. In it were an army officer and two enlisted men. One of the enlisted men spoke up, "I'm sure I saw someone run into the jungle, Sir."

"Go have a quick look, but don't take forever." Although the men spoke in Spanish, the evacuees understood the essence of what was being said by the soldiers' actions.

The soldier got out and disappeared into the forest after Koki. The officer watched for a few seconds, then closed his eyes and relaxed. Neither he nor the other man saw as Frank crept up behind the officer brandishing a log about the size and shape of a policeman's night stick. Frank swung the log at the officer knocking him unconscious. This unnerved the enlisted man and he panicked and froze. Frank saw his opportunity and grabbed the man's rifle.

Frank picked up a rope that had been stashed on the floor of the jeep. June, Danny and Ron came out of hiding. "Here you two, take the uniform off the soldier then tie him and the officer up."

June came up beside Frank, "What are we going to do about finding Koki?"

"I'll have to go look for him. Drag the two soldiers into the bushes and then you three hide. The other soldier may come back. Take this rifle."

Ron reached for the rifle, "Should we shoot him?"

"NO! Don't be shooting anyone. Just hold it on him until you get him tied up."

It only took Frank a couple of minutes to locate Koki and the other soldier. Koki was facing the soldier who was holding him at gun point. Behind Koki was a sharp drop-off. The soldier heard Frank's approach. With the butt of his rifle the soldier gave Koki a hard push over the edge. He then turned to Frank. As Frank heard the report of the rifle, he felt a burning pain in his right upper arm. Ignoring the pain, he lunged head first into the man's stomach, knocking the wind out of him. Before he could get up, Frank kicked him in the face rendering him unconscious.

"Help me, Mr. Grimes help me!"

Frank looked over the edge and saw Koki clinging to a bush about six feet down. "Hang on Koki, I'll get you." After assuring himself an overhanging tree was sturdy enough to hold him and Koki, Frank wrapped his legs around the tree and crossed his ankles. He then hung upside down and reached for Koki.

"Grab my good arm."

Koki continued to hang onto the bush with both hands disregarding Frank's help.

"Koki, you have to let go and grab me!"

"I can't, I can't. I'm going to die."

"No, you aren't. Not if you do as I say. Now grab my hand. I can't hang upside down like this forever."

Koki murmured and moaned but let go of the limb with one hand and quickly reached up for Frank's hand.

"Good, now do just as I say. Let go with your other hand and take hold of my belt." Koki hesitated for a second before doing as Frank said. "Now, let go of my hand and reach for the root next to my elbow. Put your foot in the cup of my hand, and I'll give you a boost up." Fortunately, Koki was slight in stature. Frank outweighed him by sixty or seventy pounds.

Koki did as Frank instructed. He pulled

himself over the edge to safety. Falling in a heap, he started crying hysterically.

"Koki! Koki! Buck up! I need you to help me get up."

Koki lay on the ground in a fetal position sobbing. Frank had a momentary flashback of his war experience. With one last effort, Frank yelled, "KOKI!! HELP ME!"

Koki pulled himself together long enough to grab onto Frank's legs and pull him up. He then threw his arms around Frank and cried feverishly. "I was so scared. I was sure I was dead."

Frank patted Koki's back, "I know son, I know."

Koki finally quieted down and wiped his eyes on his shirt. He looked at Frank rather embarrassed. Then he realized blood was dripping down Frank's right arm. "Mr. Grimes, you're hurt!"

Frank handed Koki a very dirty blue handkerchief. "Wrap this tight around my arm."

"But this handkerchief is dirty and it's not white."

"Just do as I say."

 **Chapter 31**

Reaching the road, Frank saw Ron sitting in the jeep fussing with the officer who had regained consciousness. A rag was stuffed and tied over his mouth. He glared at Frank.

With alarm June looked at Frank, "You're hurt. We heard a shot. What happened?"

Grinning Frank tried to make light of the situation, "As the cowboys say in the movies, 'It's only a flesh wound'. But, boy, flesh wounds sure hurt! Danny, you, and Koki take some of the rope and go tie up the man we left in the woods."

June started to fret over Frank. He sat down on the grass and told her what had happened. She got a first aid kit out of the jeep and tended to his arm. The two boys came back just as June finished bandaging the arm.

When she finished doing what she could, Frank spoke up, "Get this guy out of the jeep and let's get out of here." Danny and Ron pulled the officer out of the jeep and tossed him onto the roadside.

Danny reached into the back seat and held up a canteen, "Dad, while we were waiting for you look what I found. And Ron found a bag of food.

Koki grabbed the canteen and started to take a drink. He stopped and looked at Frank. Here, Mr. Grimes, you take a drink first."

"Thanks. One of you guys drive. I'm about done in." June helped Frank into the back seat then climbed in beside him.

Ron jumped behind the wheel, "Let me. I've always wanted to drive a jeep. Hey, look, this jeep has two brakes."

"Two brakes? What are you talking about?" Danny walked over to the driver's side to investigate.

Ron showed him, "See here's the accelerator and here are two brakes."

Frank groaned. He leaned over the seat, "Those aren't two brakes." Pointing to the peddle on the left, Frank said, "That one's a clutch. The one in the middled is the brake."

"Clutch? What's a clutch?"

Frank looked from one to the other in

disbelief, "Do any of you know how to drive a stick shift?" They just looked at Frank dumb founded.

June got out from the back, "Move over youngster and let experience take over. I cut my teeth on a '32 Chevy. Just hang on tight." The wheels spun and dirt flew as June took off. The men grabbed hold of whatever was available for safety.

The jeep had been ascending for several hours before the road started to slope downward. By now the condition of the road had improved. They rounded a bend and could see the road below. There was a bridge crossing a wide ravine. Guarding the bridge were three soldiers. June drove the jeep behind overhanging vegetation covering one side of the road. Frank ordered, "Get out. Be quiet and hide behind the stone outcropping over there."

They watched the soldiers wandering about and not paying any attention to their surroundings. Occasionally they would stop and appear to be joking with each other. Ron finally asked, "Well, what now? Do you suppose we should just take our chances and go down and ask them to let us pass?"

Koki expressed his opinion, "Somehow, I really doubt they'll just let us pass. So far, the soldiers haven't been very friendly."

Frank sighed, "Unfortunately, we can't take any chances on their willingness to help us. By now, word has probably reached them about the encounter we had earlier and our stealing a jeep."

"Frank, I have an idea." Frank and the boys looked skeptically at June. "Come on, we need to go a safe distance into the jungle, out of sight and where the soldiers can't hear us."

June was followed by the others for some distance. She appeared to be looking for something. She stopped beside a thick bush with very large leaves, "See these leaves? I've seen the women in San Marza use these to make mats by tearing them into long strips. What if we weave them all loose, not tight like they do for mats but…?

Excited, Danny all but shouted, "Loose like a net!"

"Not so loud Danny. Yes, like a net." June looked at Frank, who had a scowl on his face, "We can do it Frank!"

"I don't see what other choice we have." He looked at each of them, "Anyone have a better idea?" The young men shrugged their shoulders. "Okay then. June, tell us what to do."

"First, I suppose, we need to gather as much of this stuff as we can find."

The fellows, eager to help, took off in three different directions. Frank turned to June, "I hope they don't get lost or let the soldiers see them."

Darkness engulfed the little group with only the moon for illumination. The little army sat weaving a very loose net. It was not as difficult to weave as they had thought it would be. Frank realized it was not strong and would not hold back the soldiers for very long. But all they needed were a few minutes to get across the bridge.

"Frank, we're going to have to keep this up all night for the net to be big enough to do any good. We also need some rest. I suggest we work in shifts."

"That's a good idea. Ron is about to go to sleep already. Ron get a blanket and stretch out. June, you too. We'll wake you in a couple of hours." Ron wrapped himself in a blanket and was soon heard snoring. June lay down near Frank. She was so tired but had difficulty falling asleep. She started praying. She prayed for their safety, and safety for the soldiers. She did not want anyone to be killed. She continued to pray and slowly she drifted into slumber.

For the next two hours, Frank, Danny and Koki sat weaving the net. Koki stopped tearing the leaves into strips and softly spoke up. "Mr. Grimes?"

"What?"

"Thank you for saving my life today. I was

really scared. I don't think I have ever been more afraid in my life."

"Well, I'm sure you would have done the same for me if the situation were reversed."

"I'm not so sure. I was kind of a coward."

"It was your first encounter with something like that. And you didn't have any training in dealing with such a situation. Don't worry about it."

"What you did is kind of like what Jesus did, isn't it?

Frank stopped weaving and looked at Koki. "I'm not sure I follow you."

"Well, Jesus came to our rescue when we had no hope of saving ourselves from sin. You didn't have to help me. You chose to save my life."

"Sure, Koki."

"I know I'm very young and won't pretend I understand or know all the answers. All I know is, Jesus loves us. That means you Mr. Grimes. I know you harbor resentment for the Japanese. It's hard to let go and trust Jesus. Like it was hard for me to let go of the flimsy branch I was holding onto. It really wasn't secure. I would have fallen to my death. We hold on to the things of this world for one reason or another. We need to let go and take Jesus's hand and let Him be our Savior."

"I'm sure there's a lot of truth in what you're saying; but right now, my arm is really hurting and I'm just too tired to think about such things. I've got to get a little shut-eye." Having said this, Frank put down the net and stretched out on the grass.

He lay staring into the night. He slept only about an hour before getting up.

June and Ron took Koki's and Danny's place a couple of hours before sunrise. Frank had not slept anymore. The net was noticeably larger as June, Frank and Ron continued to weave. Ron was fighting sleep. He'd weave a few lengths then nod off. Frank purposely bumped his side to wake him. June looked at Frank with a smirk. Finally, Frank gave up and let Ron sleep.

"What do you think? The net doesn't look any too strong. Will it do the job or have we wasted our time?" June said this as she stripped another leaf. Her hands were red and swollen from stripping the leaves. She noticed Frank's hands were also covered in red welts.

"You're right, it isn't very strong. But it

really doesn't have to be. It just has to hold together long enough to confuse the soldiers while we drive across the bridge. I'd like to have time to practice running and throwing this thing with the boys. But there isn't time and probably one toss and the thing will fall apart."

"It looks just about big enough to me. What do you say?" June put down the leaf she had been tearing.

"Yup, I'd say we're about finished." Frank leaned back against a tree and rested his hands in his lap. "Koki and I had a talk last night. He's not a bad kid. I guess I've been painting all Japanese with the same brush. You know, I've never really put much thought into church or Jesus. I've been going to church just to please you."

"Yes, I know. But it has been good for the

children to see you go. And I think it has benefited you, also."

"I did do a lot of praying during the war especially for you and the kids. I don't know. I just don't know."

Before June could think of a reply to Frank, Danny woke up and came over to his parents. "Morning Mom. Dad, have you thought how we're going to pull this thing off?"

"I've been thinking about that most of the night. The soldiers have been out there all night with no relief. They're probably pretty tired and not very alert. Our biggest problem is getting them close enough together so we can catch them all under the net at once. I think our best time is as early as possible, like right now. Go wake up Koki." Having said that, Frank gave Ron a rap on the bottom of his foot as Danny went to wake Koki.

When the group was assembled and ready, Frank told them his plan. "We'll push the jeep to the center of the road just out of sight of the soldiers. June can drive. The rest of us will skirt around to the approach to the bridge. We'll wait for the three of them to come close enough together so we can throw the net over all of them at once. As soon as it looks like they're as near to each other as they will get, I'll fire a shot and we'll throw the net over them.

"June, when you hear the shot, start the motor and drive as fast as you dare towards the bridge. When you get to the bridge slow down just enough so we can hop in, then take off like lightning or at least as fast as this thing can go."

Frank stood looking at June for what

seemed an eternity. He set the net down, took June in his arms and kissed her passionately. Saying nothing, the young men stared open-mouthed.

Without the motor running and as silently as they could, the four men pushed the jeep to the center of the road. June was sitting in the driver's seat praying nervously.

Frank shifted his weight from one foot to the other. With a subtle hand motion, he quietly said, "Come on men, let's get this thing over."

June could see the soldiers and the bridge from her vantage point. The soldiers were milling around. One stretched. Another yawned repeatedly. She also spied Frank and the boys moving towards the bridge.

The men crouched as they got closer to

their target. They were now close enough to hear the soldiers talking in Spanish. Danny had taken two years of Spanish in high school and was enrolled in a Spanish class in college. Frank had picked up bits and pieces of Spanish and was able to understand some of what was being said. Neither Ron nor Koki understood any of the conversation.

"This sure has been a long night. Not one vehicle. What a waste of time. Why are we bothering to watch this bridge all night?"

"Orders are orders. Besides it's not really hard work. As long as we have to put in our time, I'd just as soon put it in this way."

The third soldier added his thoughts, "They haven't even bothered to fix our telephone or check on us. For all headquarters knows, we could all be dead. We have no idea what's happening. And I'm out of cigarettes. Will one of you give me one?"

The third soldier had been standing further away from the other two. He walked closer to them to get a cigarette that was being offered. They heard a gunshot and froze. Barreling down the road came the jeep. There was a blood-curdling scream and the net was dropped over the three soldiers.

Frank and the boys gave the soldiers a hard push to the side of the road and kept running towards the jeep. June slowed enough for the four to jump in. Ron landed face down on the back floorboard. He straightened himself up and made circles in the air as though he were swinging a lasso, "Yaah, whoo!"

Chapter 32

The evacuees reached the outskirts of San Marie late in the morning. Not sure of the situation, they had discarded the jeep and were hiding in a ditch in ankle deep water watching the comings and goings. Soldiers were everywhere, as well as colorfully dressed people. In the distance, they could see azure blue water and boats of various sizes bobbing peacefully on it. Anchored far out in the harbor was a beautiful big gunmetal gray Navy ship which although obscured by smoke and haze, appeared to be flying an American flag.

"Frank, what do you think? Do you think it's safe for us to walk into town?"

"I'm not sure, Sweetheart. Somehow, I doubt those soldiers are just going to give us a free taxi ride to the ship."

Danny agreed with his father, "Yeah, somehow, I've got the distinct feeling most of the soldiers aren't like the captain who Dad said likes 'Norteamericanos'."

Ron, ever the pessimist spoke, "I hope the ship out there is ours."

Koki frowned at Ron, "Shut up, Ron. Why wouldn't it be. It hasn't been three days yet. Look at the flag."

Frank had irritated his wound when he threw the net. He was tired and his arm was paining him terribly. He had about reached the end of his patience, "Quiet you two. Let me think."

June spoke softly, "I have an idea. Danny, do you think you can sneak up to that clothesline over there by the pink and green house without being seen? I want you to get that print dress and the shawl next to it."

"Mom! What are you thinking?"

"Yes, June, what is it you have in mind this time?"

"I can put on the dress and shawl and walk into town without anyone even giving me a second look. I'll just look like another abuela. I'll mill around and see what I can find out."

"No. I think it's too dangerous."

"Well, do any of you have a better idea? No one is going to pay me any attention." The three young men stared at the ground. Frank continued to look heartbreakingly at June. "All right then, Danny, go get the clothes."

The others watched as Danny moved surreptitiously, zigzagging his way to the clothesline. Returning with the clothes, Danny handed them to his mother. After giving them to her he hugged her tightly. "Please, be careful Mom."

"I will. Now you fellows just stay put. I'll be back before you know it."

June disappeared deeper into the underbrush. The men watched as she appeared on the road several yards beyond their hiding place. Soon she was mingling with the confused multitude.

An hour passed, then two. The men remained in hiding. No one spoke. Ron had fallen asleep. Frank, Danny and Koki impatiently watched the road. Several cars, a number of military vehicles and a couple of trucks rumbled by. Frank watched as a small canvas covered civilian truck passed them. It was driven by a large man with a heavy beard and shaggy hair. A woman sat in the passenger's seat. Startled, Frank was sure it was June. The truck went a short distance, stopped, then made a U-turn.

As the truck drove very slowly past, the woman leaned out the window. It was June! "Quick, get in the back and hide. Hurry, it's too dangerous to stop." The men scrambled to get in and hid behind various boxes.

The truck was stopped by a soldier on guard duty, as it reentered the town. June took slow deep breaths trying to control her fear. The soldier spoke in Spanish,

"What are you doing returning to town? Didn't I just see you drive out?"

"Yes, that is correct. But we only got a little way when this forgetful woman of mine said she forgot our evening meal. Our journey is long to our home and we will get very hungry. We must go back to my mother-in-law's house and pick up the food she has prepared for us to take with us."

"Yeah. Yeah. Okay, drive on."

The truck continued to maneuver through the winding traffic: motor-driven, horse-drawn and pedestrian. The late afternoon sun was beating down relentlessly, when June saw a beautiful site, far out in the harbor was the ship they had spotted from the ditch. It was flying the stars and stripes, waiting for them! The driver pulled up to the dock. June and the driver jumped out and ran to the back.

"Out, out, quickly. I do not wish to get into trouble. Out! Out!" The men jumped out. The driver turned to June as she took off her wedding rings and handed them to him.

"June, what are you doing? Those are your wedding rings."

"They are the only thing I have left to give him in exchange for the ride. I don't have any money."

"But, your wedding rings!"

"There is no security in holding on to the things of this world." She pointed out to the end of the pier, "Come on, that man in the small boat there, is going to take us out to the ship."

"What did you promise him? My ring?"

"Yes, I did."

The little haggard group started towards the pier just as a car screeched to a halt. Carlos jumped out. "Mr. and Mrs. Grimes, I finally found you!"

Frank took Carlos's hand, giving it a hardy shake, "Carlos what are you doing here?"

"When I learn of the coup, I go to your house. I want to help you get to the harbor. But you were gone. I look and look and look. Now I find you and you are safe."

June walked up to Carlos and gave him a tender, loving hug. "Carlos, oh, Carlos."

"I was afraid for you. I know you do not speak the Spanish good. I think maybe I can help you get by the guards and help you get to San Marie. But you are two smart people. You are here without my help."

June gave him another hug. "You are so

kind. We will never forget you. Give me your address. When we get back to the states, I'll write you. We can keep in touch." She then hugged him a third time and kissed him."

The worn-out group got into the boat. The weathered boatman's strong arms pulled them towards the Navy ship. Frank and June continued to wave good-bye to Carlos, as he stood on the pier waving to them with tears in his eyes.

Watching as the pier receded, June looked down at her bare hand. She could see a white ring around her finger. A parable Jesus had told came to mind. It was about a merchant looking for fine pearls. When he found one of great value, he sold everything he had and bought it.* June hadn't sold everything to buy a pearl. She had sold her precious pearl to buy freedom. She prayed it was more than just physical freedom.

***Matthew 13:45**

Chapter 33

The boat pulled up to the ship. Several sailors helped the relieved travelers up the accommodation ladder at the side of the ship. The boatman held out his hand for his payment. After trying several times, Frank finally got his ring off and gave it to the boatman. He looked at June and said, "Well, that's the last thing. We're totally broke."

Several other Americans were already on board. A sailor was assigned to take the three single men to the hanger deck where they would be bunked. Ensign DeJean was assigned to aid Frank and June. He guided them to sick-bay. There a corpsman attended to Frank's wound. The corpsman joked about it only being a "flesh wound" as in the cowboy movies. Frank gave him a weary glare before saying, "That line has already been used."

Ensign DeJean gave the corpsman a cautioning look before leading the Grimes to a state room in Officers' Country. When June asked if they were putting an officer out of his room Ensign DeJean replied, "No ma'am. We were in port in Rio De Janeiro, Brazil. Two thirds of the crew were on liberty, as was usual. When we received orders to get underway, the shore patrol was sent to find and bring the men back. Two officers and four enlisted men couldn't be located before we pulled out."

"Will they be in trouble?"

"No, they shouldn't be. That is if they report

to the Senior Officer Present Afloat. They'll be assigned something to do until we return to pick them up."

Ensign DeJean asked them if they would like to use the 'head'. When June looked at him confused, he chuckled and said it was the Navy term for bathroom. "Give me a rough idea of your sizes. I'll find something clean for you to wear and get the clothes you're wearing laundered. You'll have them back by tomorrow." Having finished getting June and Frank settled, Ensign DeJean left.

The ship was soon underway to everyone's relief. The rescued Americans totaled fifteen adults and six children. They were served supper on the Mess Decks where the enlisted men ate. The meal consisted of roast pork, whipped potatoes with gravy, peas, bread, a salad, pudding, coffee and what the sailors referred to as "bug juice", an artificially citrus-flavored sweetened drink. The meal was served on divided tin trays. The children wondered why there was a raised edge on the table. A sailor explained it was to prevent the trays from sliding off the table when waves caused the ship to tip. Just as he finished talking, they felt a little tipping. The sailor smiled and said, "See what I mean?"

Everyone was expected to carry his own tray to the Scullery for cleaning. Most of the group were very fatigued and went to bed directly after supper.

Sunrise broke bright and gusty. The ship's 'guests' were rudely awakened by announcements on a loud speaker. They had been so tired the night before most had not been aware of it. Civilians intermingled with sailors around the decks.

Koki was encircled by a group of sailors. "Yep, that's really what happened. I'll never forget Mr. Grimes. He is one fine man. He saved my life…"

Frank and June stood off to the side, listening, but out of sight of Koki. Frank smiled and looked up at the blue sky. He leaned towards June and put his good arm around her, kissing her on the temple.

"June, I know God had something to do with all of this. It was His way of getting my attention. Probably this was His way of waking me up and having me see what's really important. You know we've lost everything?"

"Yes, I know. Pastor Haas preached a sermon once about things. He said, 'Don't hold on to things too tightly. Because it won't hurt as much when God pries your fingers open to wrest them out of your hand'." June leaned into Frank's good shoulder.

"I want to tell you something." He looked down into June's loving eyes, "I knew all along you didn't want to come here. I'm sorry. It's my fault we lost our home."

"It's alright. I'd rather be with you in the littlest shack anywhere in the world than alone in a vast mansion."

Frank again kissed June on her temple. "I don't know what's wrong with me. I'm like a dog with a bone. My whole life, whenever I've gotten hold of something, I just couldn't let go and move on, even when I realized I was wrong. Like when we first got married and I kept bringing up Millicent. I knew that wasn't right. And when I came home from the war, I held on to my bitter, hateful feelings. I didn't want to let them go. And the first day we reached San Marza, I knew I had made a mistake, insisting we come down here. But I just couldn't admit it."

June looked up at Frank, "I knew you were miserable. I just didn't know how to reach you."

"Yesterday, while you were in town finding help for us, I finally did let go. I prayed like I've never prayed before. At first it was for your safety. I told God I didn't want to live without you. God whispered to me. He said if I would let go and turn my life over to Him, no matter what happened, we could always be together because 'always' would be eternity."

Frank stopped talking, turned, and looked at June eye to eye. June continued to look at him with hope in her teary eyes. "I asked God to forgive me of all I've done wrong and to be my Savior. Now I need to go to Koki and ask for his forgiveness for treating him so poorly. Actually, there is probably a long list of people back home who I could go to, to ask their forgiveness. And tell them about the change God has made in my life."

June smiled at Frank with the tears in her eyes washing down her cheeks waiting for him to continue. "I felt so clean inside after I prayed. The hate and shame were gone. I wish I'd done it sooner."

"Oh Frank!" June put her arms around his mid-section and squeezed him as tight as she could.

"Hey, be careful, you're going to break a rib! You know that doesn't change the fact we are totally broke. We don't have anything."

June's heart soared to heaven with praise, "We have what matters most!"

Ron came through a hatch from a passage-way onto the deck and saw Frank and June. He was carrying the uniform Frank had previously told him to take from the soldier. It was now perfectly clean. It had been thrown in with the rest of the dirty laundry. "Hey, Mr. Grimes what am I supposed to do with this uniform?"

"Keep it as a souvenir, wear it as a Halloween costume, throw it overboard. I really don't care." Ron looked at it one last time then pitched it into the water.

"Frank, why did you tell Ron to take the uniform in the first place?"

"I'm not sure. I guess I thought we might use it somehow."

The ship returned to Rio De Janeiro. The United States Counsel gave the refugees unlimited use of telephones and loaned money to those who needed it, to fly to the states. They all flew to Miami, Florida. Rusty was waiting for them when they disembarked. June was surprised and happy to see her older son. After hugs and greetings, Rusty said he had news that just couldn't wait. June thought maybe that after five years of marriage, Rusty and Shelby were finally going to be parents.

Before Rusty had a chance to tell them the good news Koki approached them accompanied by his parents. "Mr. and Mrs. Grimes, I would like to introduce you to my parents., Mr. and Mrs. Yonai." His parents bowed as they were introduced.

Frank took Koki's father's hand, shaking it warmly. He held on to it saying, Mr. Yonai, I want you to know what a fine son you have raised. You have much to be proud of." Mr. Yonai thanked Frank. Then Frank turned to Koki, "Koki, I want to apologize to you. I mistreated you for reasons that were none of your fault. Please forgive me."

Koki was flabbergasted at what Frank had just said. "Mr. Grimes, we were both in error in some of our actions. I want you to know how much I admire you. I've decided to inquire about R.O.T.C. when I return to college. I want to be as capable handling difficult situations as you are." It was Frank's turn to be flabbergasted.

Rusty could wait no longer. "Dad, listen to me. Remember when Shelby and I got married? You loaned us money to buy some land. I insisted we put the deed in both our names until I could pay you back."

"Sure, I remember. Mom and I meant it as a gift, not a loan. However, I did think the land was worthless. Tell me gold was found on it."

"Not exactly. It has black gold. Oil."

"Oil! How much?"

"Not so much that you're rich. But there's enough so you're not going to have to worry about money for the rest of your life."

Frank sat down on a nearby bench. June sat beside him and put her arm around his shoulders. They looked at each other with tears in their eyes and laughed. It now wasn't relevant if they were rich or poor. They had found the secret of what matters most.

The End

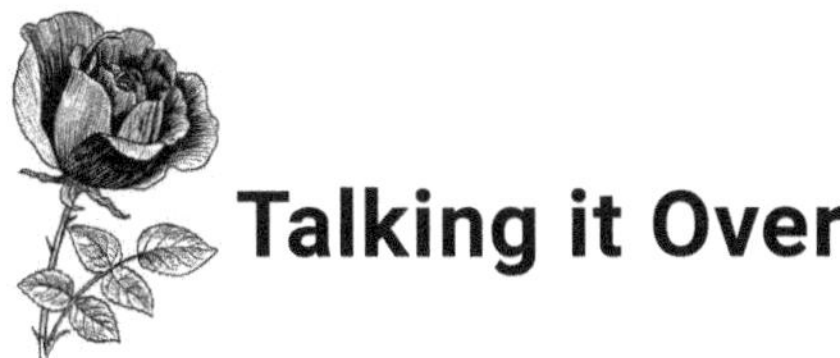 **Talking it Over**

CHAPTER 2

- June married out of her social and economic class. What could she and Frank have done to prepare each other for this change?

- It was customary in the era of the story for the groom to make the honeymoon decisions. What would you do if you were in a situation, either in your marriage, at work or some other group setting, where someone else made all the decisions, and they weren't all that good?

- Ruth, June's sister-in-law, had briefly met June the day before. Ruth assumed June was a Christian and familiar with Vacation Bible School. Tell of a time or situation you were in, when someone assumed you knew more than you did. How did you handle it?

CHAPTER 5

- Hilda was brutally honest regarding her son's obsession with his first wife and the condition of the house. When is it proper for someone to be forthright about a situation?

CHAPTER 6

- What is the best way to talk to someone about becoming a Christian?

CHAPTER 7

- June had to address Frank's obsession with the memory of Millicent. List ways spouses or sweethearts can be obsessed. Tell how you would manage the situation.

- Della Whitherspoon, June's mother, had to live her whole life knowing she had caused the death of her sister. After this accident how could this tragedy have been better handled?

CHAPTER 8

- God caused the clouds to cover the moon. Tell of a divine intervention in your life?

CHAPTER 10

- Why do you think June never told anyone about Donna Vandenburg offering her a ride?

CHAPTER 11

- As a new bride June wanted to have the Thanksgiving dinner at her house. Tell of a time you felt compelled to do something?

- What do you think Charles Whitherspoon might have said to his sons?

- What do you think about June feeling she had to ask her husband before accepting a full-time teaching position?

CHAPTER 12

- Tell why you think Eddie Stover should have been arrested. Or tell why you think June made the right decision. List an event in your life when something happened that was not black or white.

CHAPTER 15

- The Grimes felt secure. They had a lovely home with two children. Frank had a good job and didn't believe he would be drafted. They thought they were 'home free.' Tell of a time in your life when you thought you were 'home free.' What happened? How did you handle it?

CHAPTER 16

- What do you think Art, Duke and Barney told Gaylen Browne on the night of their visit?

CHAPTER 18

- What was the root cause of Frank's inability to readjust to civilian life?

CHAPTER 19

- What do you think it was about Rev. Haas that got Frank to come every week?

CHAPTER 20

- What would have been a better solution to the problem with Vivi getting hurt than throwing away the roller skates and forbidding playing the game?

CHAPTER 21

- At the same time Frank was interviewing for a lesser paying job, June was being offered a teaching position. Name a time when God answered a problem before you had even prayed about it.

CHAPTER 22

- June felt so deeply about Frank's situation that she told God she would do whatever it would take to help him find peace. Tell of a similar situation you have experienced.

CHAPTER 24

- June adapted to life in San Marza. What would you have done?

CHAPTER 25-26

- How do you react when uninvited guests come to your house?

CHAPTER 27

- It is important to talk about your family's Christian history, even if the history begins with you. What would your history include?

CHAPTER 30

- Frank hated the Japanese people. But he risked his life to save Koki. What would you do if someone abused you and later needed you to help?

- June gave the last thing she had, her wedding rings, to save the evacuees.

What would you be willing to give up so you could be saved?

CHAPTER 31

- Koki related how Frank saving him was analogous to Jesus saving us. Tell of a time when you have compared an event to Jesus's salvation.

CHAPTER 32

- What do you think about the idea that the Grimes had to lose everything before Frank realized what mattered most?

CHAPTER 33

- Finding oil on land partly owned by Frank and June could be called 'A God Wink,' otherwise known as a blessing. Have you ever experienced a God wink?

Acknowledgments

It is with utmost gratitude that I dedicated this book to my incredible husband, John. It was because of his encouragement, moral support, and contribution that brought this story to fruition. He suggested realistic detail for several situations. He provided personal expertise from his Navy service. He listened patiently to my ramblings. John should really be listed as co-author. I have been blessed to have been married to him for over sixty years.

This is the third book the Typewriter Creative Co. has published for me. They are an extraordinary group of ladies. Taryn,

MaryBeth, Cassidy, Sara and Janna are committed to creating a quality product. I have been so pleased with their efforts and proud of the finished books.

Photograph on the cover is Marsha Pester's mother,
Catherine Delong Sabin, taken around 1941.

About the Author

Marsha began writing after retiring from a career in nursing and teaching school. She lives in Joliet, Illinois with John, her husband of sixty years.